Rotherham Libraries and Neighbourhood Hubs

'Long-time readers of Levy's work will know that she's just as capable of voyaging into the surreal and uncanny as she is documenting the social and psychological mores of her characters . . . you have a sense of a writer who's capable of nearly anything . . . a writer whose work has crossed boundaries of format and genre' *Longreads*

'Reading Deborah Levy's novels is a lesson in humility. She is a careful and intelligent writer with an absolute command of language, one who demands you not only to pay close attention, but also second-guess your immediate reactions and responses to her work. Her novels are deceptively slim in length, but supersized with profound ideas that defy preconceived notions and easy interpretations. *The Man Who Saw Everything* is just such a book, and reading it is the best possible sort of challenge' *Newsday*

'A superbly crafted, enigmatic new story from an author of note. In a relatively short book, Levy spins an extraordinary web of connection, a dreamscape in which plangent images like a pearl necklace, a spilled drink or the petals of a tree recur like soft chimes. Head-spinning and playful yet translucent, Levy's writing offers sophistication and delightful artistry. Levy defies gravity in a daring, time-bending new novel' *Kirkus*

'Booker-Prize-finalist Levy explores the fragile connections and often vast chasms between self and others in this playful, destabilizing, and consistently surprising novel . . . Levy's novel brilliantly explores the parallels between personal and political history, and prompts questions about how one sees oneself – and what others see' *Publishers Weekly*

'*The Man Who Saw Everything* is bifurcated into two time periods: 1988 and 2016, but by Deborah Levy's deft hand and brilliant command of metaphor, the boundaries of space and time collapse. This is an extraordinary novel that captures the zeitgeist and spectres of twentieth-century Communism in such a way that far exceeds the 200 pages it is bound in' *Shelf Awareness*

'An evocative journey across a shapeshifting personal and political landscape. As Levy peels back each new layer of this at-times enigmatic story, there are new pleasures disclosed at every turn' *Bookpage*

'There is no way to succinctly summarize this slim book and adequately convey how it manages to hold exquisitely actual multiverses within its pages. A brilliant, blistering, bold look at identity, relationships and time; a perfect puzzle of a novel' *Nylon*

ABOUT THE AUTHOR

Deborah Levy is a British novelist and poet. She is the author of seven novels: *Beautiful Mutants*, *Swallowing Geography*, *The Unloved*, *Billy & Girl*, *Swimming Home*, *Hot Milk* and *The Man Who Saw Everything*. *Swimming Home* was shortlisted for the Man Booker Prize 2012; *Hot Milk* was shortlisted for the Man Booker Prize 2016 and the Goldsmiths Prize 2016; and *The Man Who Saw Everything* was longlisted for the Booker Prize 2019 and shortlisted for the Goldsmiths Prize 2019. Deborah is also the author of an acclaimed collection of short stories, *Black Vodka*, and two 'living autobiographies', *Things I Don't Want to Know* and *The Cost of Living*. She has written for the Royal Shakespeare Company and is a Fellow of the Royal Society of Literature.

THE MAN WHO SAW EVERYTHING

Deborah Levy

PENGUIN BOOKS

PENGUIN BOOKS

UK | USA | Canada | Ireland | Australia
India | New Zealand | South Africa

Penguin Books is part of the Penguin Random House group of companies
whose addresses can be found at global.penguinrandomhouse.com.

First published by Hamish Hamilton 2019
Published in Penguin Books 2020
002

Copyright © Deborah Levy, 2019

The moral right of the author has been asserted

Printed and bound in Great Britain by Clays Ltd, Elcograf S.p.A.

A CIP catalogue record for this book is available from the British Library

ISBN: 978-0-241-97760-6

www.greenpenguin.co.uk

Poetic thought, unlike rootless orchids, did not grow in a greenhouse and did not faint when confronted with today's traumas.

Karel Teige,
The Shooting Gallery (1946)

To photograph people is to violate them, by seeing them as they never see themselves, by having knowledge of them they can never have; it turns people into objects that can be symbolically possessed.

Susan Sontag, 'In Plato's Cave',
from *On Photography* (1977)

It's like this, Saul Adler: when I was twenty-three I loved the way you touched me, but when the afternoon slipped in and you slipped out of me, you were already looking for someone else. No, it's like this, Jennifer Moreau: I loved you every night and every day, but you were scared of my love and I was scared of my love, too. No, she said, I was scared of your envy, which was bigger than your love. Attention, Saul Adler. Attention! Look to the left and to the right, cross the road and get to the other side.

Abbey Road, London, September 1988

I was thinking about how Jennifer Moreau had told me I was never to describe her beauty, not to her, or to anyone else. When I asked her why I was silenced in this way, she said, 'Because you only have old words to describe me.' This was on my mind when I stepped on to the zebra crossing with its black-and-white stripes at which all vehicles must stop to allow pedestrians to cross the road. A car was coming towards me but it did not stop. I had to jump backwards and fell on my hip, using my hands to protect myself from the fall. The car stalled and a man rolled down the window. He was in his sixties, silver hair, dark eyes, thin lips. He asked if I was okay. When I did not answer he stepped out of his car.

'I apologize,' he said. 'You walked on to the crossing and I slowed down, preparing to stop, but then you changed your mind and walked back to the kerb.' His eyelids were quivering at the corners. 'And then without warning you lurched forward on to the crossing.'

I smiled at his careful reconstruction of history, blatantly told in his favour. He furtively glanced at his car to check if it had been damaged. The wing mirror had shattered. His thin lips parted and he sighed sorrowfully, muttering something about how he had ordered the mirror from Milan.

I had been up all night writing a lecture on the psychology of male tyrants and I'd made a start with the way Stalin flirted with women by flicking bread at them across the dinner table. My notes, about five sheets of paper, had fallen out of my leather sling bag and, embarrassingly, so had a packet of condoms. I started to pick them up. A small, flat, rectangular object was lying in the road. I noticed the driver was looking at my knuckles as I handed him the object, which felt warm and seemed to be vibrating in my palm. It was not mine so I assumed it was his. Blood dripped through my fingers. My palms were grazed and there was a cut on the knuckle of my left hand. I sucked it while he watched me, clearly distressed.

'Do you need a lift somewhere?'

'I'm okay.'

He offered to take me to a pharmacy to 'clean up the wound', as he put it. When I shook my head, he reached out his hand and touched my hair, which was strangely comforting. He asked for my name.

'Saul Adler. Look, it's just a small graze. I have thin skin. I always bleed a lot, it's nothing.'

He was holding his left arm in a strange way, cradling it with his right arm. I picked up the condoms and shoved them into my jacket pocket. A wind was up. The leaves that had been swept into small piles under the trees were blowing across the road. The driver told me the traffic had been diverted because there was a demonstration that day in London, and he'd wondered if Abbey Road was closed off. The detour was not signposted clearly. He did not understand why he'd become confused, because he often came this way to watch the cricket at Lord's, nearby. While he spoke, he gazed at the rectangular object in his hand.

The object was speaking. There was definitely a voice inside it, a man's voice, and he was saying something angry and insulting. We both pretended not to hear his words.

Fuck off I hate you don't come home

'How old are you, Soorl? Can you tell me where you live?'

I think the near collision had really scared the driver.

When I told him I was twenty-eight, he didn't believe me and asked

4

for my age again. He was so posh he pronounced my name as if a pebble had been inserted between the roof of his mouth and his lower lip. His silver hair was slicked back with a product that made it shine.

I in turn asked for his name.

'Wolfgang,' he said very quickly, as if he did not want me to remember it.

'Like Mozart,' I said, and then, rather like a child showing his father where he'd been hurt after falling off a swing, I pointed to the cut on my knuckle and kept repeating that I was okay. His concerned tone was starting to make me tearful. I wanted him to drive off and leave me alone. Perhaps the tears were to do with my father's recent death, though my father was not as groomed or as gentle as shiny, silver-haired Wolfgang. To hasten his departure, I explained that my girlfriend was about to arrive any minute now, so he didn't have to hang around. In fact she was going to take a photograph of me stepping on to the zebra crossing in the style of the photograph on the Beatles album.

'Which album is that, Soorl?'

'It's called *Abbey Road*. Everyone knows that. Where have you been, Wolfgang?'

He laughed but he looked sad. Perhaps it was because of the insulting words that had been spoken from inside the vibrating object in his hand.

'And how old is your girlfriend?'

'Twenty-three. Actually, *Abbey Road* was the last album the Beatles recorded together at the EMI studios, which are just over there.' I pointed to a large white house on the other side of the road.

'Of course, I know that,' he said sadly. 'It's nearly as famous as Buckingham Palace.' He walked back to his car, murmuring, 'Take care, Soorl. You're lucky to have such a young girlfriend. By the way, what do you do?'

His comments and questions were starting to irritate me – also the way he sighed, as if he carried the weight of the world on the shoulders of his beige cashmere coat. I decided not to reveal that I was a historian and that my subject was communist Eastern Europe.

It was a relief to hear the animal growl of his engine revving as I stepped back on the pavement.

Considering it was he who had nearly run me over, perhaps it was he who should take care. I waved to him but he did not wave back. As for my young girlfriend, I was only five years older than Jennifer, so what was he going on about? And why did he want to know her age? Or what I 'do'.

Never mind. I was looking at the notes in my hand (which was still bleeding), in which I had transcribed how Stalin's father had been an alcoholic and was abusive to his family. Stalin's mother had enrolled her son Joseph into a Greek orthodox priesthood school to protect him from his father's rage after he had tried to strangle her. I could not easily read my own writing but I had underlined something about how Stalin would go on to punish people for their unconscious sins as well as their conscious sins – such as thought crimes against the party.

My left hip began to ache.

Take care, Soorl. Thanks for the advice, Wolfgang.

Back to my notes, which were now smudged with blood from my knuckle. Joseph Stalin (I had written this late at night) was always pleased to punish someone. He even bullied his own son – with such cruelty that he attempted to shoot himself. His wife also shot herself, more successfully than her son, who, unlike his mother, lived to be bullied again and again by his father. My own late father was not exactly a bully. He left that task to my brother, Matthew, who was always up for a bit of cruelty. Like Stalin, Matthew went after his own family, or made sure he made their lives so miserable they went after themselves.

I sat on the wall outside the EMI studios while I waited for Jennifer to arrive. In three days I was travelling to East Germany, the GDR, to research cultural opposition to the rise of fascism in the 1930s at the Humboldt University. Although my German was reasonably fluent they had assigned me a translator. His name was Walter Müller. I was to stay for two weeks in East Berlin with his mother and sister, who had offered me a room in their tenement apartment near the university. Walter Müller was part of the reason I had nearly been run over on the zebra crossing. He had written to say that his sister, whose name was Katrin – but the family called her Luna – was a big Beatles fan. Since the 1970s, albums by both the Beatles and Bob Dylan had been allowed to be released in the GDR, unlike in the '50s and '60s, when pop music was seen by the ruling socialist party of Germany as a cultural weapon to corrupt the young. Officials were obliged to study all the lyrics before albums could be released.

Yeah yeah yeah. What could that possibly mean? What was it that was being said yes to?

It had been Jennifer's idea to take a photograph of myself crossing the zebra on Abbey Road to give to Luna. The week before she had asked me to explain the whole concept of the GDR to her but I had become distracted. We were caramelizing peanuts in the kitchen of her flat at the time and I was burning the sugar. It was quite a complicated recipe in which we were instructed to add the peanuts to the boiling sugar syrup and then bake them in the oven. Jennifer did not understand how the people of a whole country could be locked up behind a wall and not be allowed to leave. While I was banging on about how Germany came to be ideologically and physically separated into two countries divided by a wall, communist in the East, capitalist in the West, and how the communist authorities called the Wall the 'anti-fascist protection rampart', her fingers had slipped under the waistband of my jeans. I was burning the sugar and Jennifer was not exactly taking notes. We had both lost interest in the German Democratic Republic.

I saw her walking towards me carrying a small aluminium stepladder on her arm. She was wearing the Soviet pilot's cap I had bought her at a flea market on the Portobello Road. I kissed her and told her briefly what had happened. Jennifer was preparing for an exhibition of her photographs at art school, but had taken the afternoon off to do the 'photo shoot', as she called it. Some sort of camera was strapped to her leather belt; another hung around her neck. I did not disclose the details of the near crash, but she noticed the cut on my knuckle. 'You've got thin skin,' she said. I asked her why she was carrying a stepladder. She told me that was how the original photo of the Beatles on the Abbey Road zebra crossing was taken in August 1969 at 11.30 a.m. The photographer, Iain MacMillan, had placed the ladder at the side of the zebra while a policeman was paid to direct the traffic. MacMillan was given ten minutes to take the photo. But as I was not actually famous in any way, we couldn't ask the police for five minutes so we had to work quickly.

'I think there's been a diversion and Abbey Road is closed today.'

As I was speaking three cars sped by, followed by a black taxi for hire, a motorbike, two bicycles, and a lorry loaded with wooden planks.

'Yeah, Saul, it's definitely closed,' she said, fiddling with her camera.

'I reckon you look more like Mick Ronson than any of the Beatles, even though your hair is black and Mick's is blond.'

It was true that my hair, which was shoulder-length, had been cut by Jennifer two days ago in the style of Bowie's lead guitarist. She was secretly proud of what she called my rock-star looks, and she loved my body more than I loved my body, which made me love her.

When the road was clear she set up the ladder in the same place that Wolfgang was supposed to have stopped his car. As she clambered up and sorted out her camera, she yelled instructions: 'Put your hands in your jacket pockets! Look down! Look straight ahead! Okay, walk now! Bigger strides! Go!' There were two cars waiting but she held up her hand to keep them there as she put a new roll of film into her camera. When the cars started to hoot, she flamboyantly bowed to them from the top of the ladder.

To thank Jennifer for her time, I bought six oysters from the fish-monger and a bottle of dry white. We spent the next couple of hours in her bed while her two flatmates, Saanvi and Claudia, were out. It was a poky, dark basement flat, but they all enjoyed living there and seemed to get along. Claudia was a vegan who was always soaking some sort of seaweed in a bowl of water in the kitchen.

When we kissed fully clothed on the bed, her pilot cap kept fall-ing over her eyes, which really turned me on. Now and again blue lights flashed in my head, but I didn't tell Jennifer, who was playing with the string of pearls I always wore around my neck. When I finally took off my white trousers, she noticed that I had a large bruise on my right thigh and both my knees were grazed and bleeding.

'Can you tell me what actually happened, Saul?'

I told her more about how I had nearly been run over just before she arrived and how I was embarrassed about picking up the packet of condoms. She laughed and then slurped an oyster and threw the shell on the floor.

'We should look for pearls inside those oysters,' she said. 'Maybe we could make you another necklace?'

She wanted to know why I was so keen to go to East Germany, what with its citizens stuck behind that wall and the Stasi spying on everyone. Perhaps it wasn't a safe place to visit. Why didn't I do my research in West Berlin so she could visit me and we could go to concerts and drink cheap beer?

I'm not sure Jennifer truly believed I was a scholar and not a rock star.

'Your eyes are so blue,' she said, climbing on top of me and sitting astride my hips. 'It's quite unusual to have intense black hair and even more intense blue eyes. You are much prettier than I am. I want your cock inside me all the time. Everyone is frightened in the GDR aren't they? I still don't understand how the people of a whole country can be locked up behind a wall and not be allowed to leave.'

I could smell the sweet ylang-ylang oil she always combed through her hair before she walked into the tiny sauna that had come with the basement flat in Hamilton Terrace. Some nights I would arrive there from work in the evening and listen to her talking with Claudia and Saanvi in the sauna, while I marked my students' essays at the kitchen table. When Jennifer finally emerged from the sauna, sometimes an hour later, naked and oiled with her homemade ylang-ylang potion, she often tormented me by withholding her affection, making camomile tea, buttering a crispbread, then she pounced. I couldn't have wished for a more ravishing predator to pull me away from an essay in which my worst male student had ended by attributing some of the most famous lines in the world to the wrong author.

'The proletarians have nothing to lose but their chains. They have a whole world to win.'

I crossed out Leon Trotsky and wrote Karl Marx.

I knew that Jennifer was turned on by my body, but I got the impression (as she guided my fingers to touch her in the places that most thrilled her) that she was not that interested in my mind. She started to tell me how artists like Claude Cahun and Cindy Sherman meant more to her than Stalin and Erich Honecker ('No,' she said, 'here, here,' and I could feel her coming), after which she lay by my side (as I guided her fingers to the places that most pleased me) while she explained that she preferred Sylvia Plath to Karl Marx, though she liked the line in *The Communist Manifesto* about a spectre haunting Europe. 'I mean' – she was whispering now – 'usually a ghost just haunts a house or a castle, but Marx's ghost was haunting a whole continent. Maybe the spectre was standing under the Trevi Fountain in Rome to cool off from the slog of being a haunter, or buying some bling in the Versace stores in Milan, or watching a Nico concert?' Did I know that Nico's real name was Christa (I did not want to know that right now) and that Nico/Christa, who was born in Cologne, was haunted all her life by the sound of the bombing in the war? Nor did I want to know (and Jennifer stopped touching me at an erotically fierce moment to reach this thought) that a spectre was inside every photograph she developed in the dark room, and I did not recall the scene she liked in the film *Wings of Desire* (which we had recently seen together) where one of the angels says he wants 'to enter the history of the world', but now, she said, she wanted me to be the spectre inside her.

We had quite vigorous sex and afterwards I really began to ache. It was clear that something was wrong with my hip, which wasn't bruised at all.

We lazed around and finished the bottle of wine and talked. After a while Jennifer asked me what I most wanted in life.

'I would like to see my mother again.'

It wasn't the sexiest answer, but I knew it would interest Jennifer.

'Then perhaps you should visit her.'

'You know she's dead.'

'Go to your family house in Bethnal Green and tell me what happens.'

She had found a stick of charcoal and was balancing a sheet of paper across her naked thighs.

'I can see cobblestones and a Gothic university,' I said.

Her hand did not move across the page.

'I thought you were going to draw?'

'Well, there isn't a Gothic university in Bethnal Green. I'd rather draw your mother than a building. Do you miss her more than your father?'

It was hard work being tangled up with someone like Jennifer Moreau. We heard the front door slam.

'That will be Claudia.' Jennifer placed my hand in the middle of the sheet of paper and drew around my fingers with the stick of charcoal. Her bedroom was next to the kitchen and we could hear Claudia filling the kettle.

I was lying on my back and could see a bunch of flowering nettles on Jennifer's green Mexican desk in the corner of the room (made from wormwood, or something that sounded sinister), also her passport, also a pile of black-and-white photographs. I wanted to tell Jennifer that I loved her, but I thought it might put her off me.

The bedroom door suddenly creaked open. Claudia, who always soaked seaweed overnight, was naked because she was about to step into the sauna, a pink towel wrapped around her head. She was yawning, slowly, massively, languorously, as if the whole world bored her shitless, one arm stretched above her head while her left hand rested on her flat tanned stomach.

I asked Jennifer Moreau if she would consider marrying me. In that moment I felt as if I had just split an atom. She leaned forward and followed my gaze.

'You know, I think it's over between us, Saul. We should call it a day, but I'll send you the Abbey Road photos anyway. Have a good time in East Berlin. I hope it works out with your visa.'

She lay back on the pillow next to me and pulled the pilot cap over her face so she did not have to look at me.

I stepped out of bed, slightly drunk, and closed the dodgy bedroom door, tripping over the empty bottle of wine we had thrown on to the scratched floorboards.

'Your white suit is on the chair,' she said. 'Can you get dressed quickly? I have to get into the dark room at college before they lock it tonight.'

I had bought the suit at Laurence Corner, the army surplus store on the Euston Road. It was where the Beatles had found their *Sergeant Pepper* jackets in the 1960s. I think my white suit used to be a Navy uniform, which was just as well because my marriage proposal had sunk to the bottom of the sea. I was shipwrecked amongst the empty oyster shells with their jagged sharp edges and I could taste Jennifer Moreau on my fingers and lips. When I perched next to her on the bed and asked her why she was suddenly so angry with me, she did not seem to know, or understand, or care. She was calm and rather cold, I thought, as if she had been thinking about this for a while.

'Well, apart from anything else, you have never once asked me about my art.'

'What do you mean?' I was shouting now. 'There's your art, it's on your walls, there and there.' I pointed to two collages taped on the wall of her room. One of them was a blown-up black-and-white photograph of my face in profile, hung above the bed like a religious icon. She had traced over the outline of my lips in red felt-tip and written the words *DON'T KISS ME*.

'I look at your art all the time.' I was still shouting. 'I think about it and I think about you. I am interested.'

'Well, seeing as you're so interested, what am I working on now?'

'I don't know, you haven't told me.'

'You haven't asked. So, what kind of camera do I use?'

She knew I had no idea. It was not as if Jennifer had much interest in communist Eastern Europe either. I mean, she hadn't exactly asked me for a reading list and I didn't hold it against her.

'Oh yes,' I said, 'you took a negative of me and taped it on your shoulder and lay in the sun and then you peeled it off and you had a sort of tattoo of me on your skin.'

She laughed. 'It's always about you, isn't it?'

In a way it was. After all, Jennifer Moreau was always taking photographs of me.

When the bedroom door creaked open again, Claudia was eating baked beans from the tin with a giant spoon.

'Jennifer' – I was pleading now – 'I'm sorry. Since my father died I've just been trying to get through the day.'

We could hear the hiss of the kettle boiling on the other side of the door.

'As it happens,' she said, jumping out of bed and slamming the door shut again, 'a curator from America came to my studio and bought two of my photographs. And she has offered me an artist's residency in Cape Cod, Massachusetts, after I graduate.'

So that's why her passport was lying on her desk.

'Congratulations,' I said miserably.

She looked so excited and young and mean. We had been together for just over a year but I knew I had met my match. For a start, the deal that Jennifer Moreau (French father, English mother, born in Beckenham, South London) had made with me was that she could praise my own sublime beauty (as she put it) in any way she liked, the shape of my body, my 'intense blue eyes', but I was never to describe her own body, or express my admiration for it, except with touch. That is how she wanted to know everything I felt and thought about her.

Claudia had now switched off the wailing kettle. When I glanced at the wall again I noticed a photograph of Saanvi taped to the crumbling plaster. The basement flat was damp and some sort of fungus crept like deranged ants over the walls of Jennifer's bedroom. In the photograph, Saanvi lay sweating on her side in the sauna. She was reading a book, her left nipple pierced with a small golden hoop.

'Get going, Saul. I don't know why you're still hanging around.'

Jennifer slipped on a kimono with a dragon embroidered on the back and then edged her feet into her favourite sandals, which were made from car tyres.

She was practically pushing me out of the door.

*

14

I spent some time fiddling with the latch on the front gate. I never could get in or out of that gate; I had watched Jennifer and Claudia leap over it on days they were late for class. Their other flatmate, Saanvi, had no problem with the latch because she was patient, but Jennifer said that was because she had a degree in Advanced Mathematics and knew a lot about limitless time.

The late-afternoon sunshine felt harsh on my eyes. My intense blue eyes. I suddenly turned around because I intuited that Jennifer was watching me. And she was. With a camera in her hand. She was standing by the front door in her dragon kimono and sandals made from car tyres, still flushed from making love with me, her left hand rummaging in her silk pockets, searching for the jelly beans she always kept there. Her camera was pointed at me. As it whirred and clicked, she said, quite dramatically, 'So long, Saul. You'll always be my muse.'

For a moment I thought she was going to throw me a jelly bean in the way that circus trainers throw treats to their performing animals after they have jumped through a flaming hoop.

'I'll get the Abbey Road photos to you before you leave. I'm sorry about your father. Hope you feel better soon, and don't forget the tinned pineapple for your translator.'

Abbey Road was a twelve-minute walk from Hamilton Terrace. Something compelled me to return to the site of the near accident. I would have to take it slowly because I noticed I was limping and that my white jacket was torn at the shoulder. Jennifer Moreau was ruthless and she seemed to know a lot about my life. How did she know that Walter Müller had requested I bring a tin of pineapple with me to the GDR? I couldn't remember if it was because I had told her or she'd asked. It was true that she had accompanied me to my father's funeral three weeks ago, so she knew about his death. Her own father had died when she was twelve, as had my mother. We often talked about losing a parent at the same age. It was a bond between us, though she thought she was freed by her father's death because he

15

would never have allowed her to go to art school. I'm not sure that I was freed by my mother's death. No, I couldn't see anything good about it, except that I never doubted her love for me, which made her absence even more of a catastrophe. All the same, my father's funeral was a reminder of Jennifer's own early loss and I had felt protective of her. My callous brother, Matthew, also known as Fat Matt (a full English breakfast seven days a week – three English eggs, three English sausages), had arranged the funeral service without consulting me.

I had been proud to have glamorous Jennifer Moreau on my arm, what with her exotic French surname, vintage powder-blue trouser suit and matching suede platform boots. I had watched Fat Matt and his shabby wife and their two young sons sitting in the front pew like they were the royals of the family, and wondered what it was that I had done so wrong in their eyes, apart from wearing a pearl necklace.

I was minor family, it seemed: unmarried, no children, relegated to the second row. It was a reminder of the crashing loneliness of my teenage years when Matt, who was not yet fat, and a Bolshevik hero in my father's eyes, started working as an electrician, earning good money while I was trying out the tester eyeliner pencils in the local chemist. By the time I got to Cambridge University he knew how to rewire a whole house while I was perfecting ways to disguise my ignorance (intense blue eyes help this endeavour) and make the most of being the raven-haired working-class cat (no claws, high cheekbones) amongst the posh pigeons.

Matt gave a loving tribute to our father. When it was my turn all I could say, as the most educated person in the family, was 'Goodbye, Dad.'

My brother did agree, though, to my idea of taking a portion of our communist father's ashes with me to be buried in the GDR. After all, he believed in it.

I glanced at the tall Edwardian villas that lined either side of Hamilton Terrace as I limped down the long, wide road, still trying to remember how Jennifer knew about the tin of pineapple I had been instructed to purchase by Walter Müller. Had she read his letter to me? Stasi informers were known as ears and eyes, *Horch und Guck*. It would seem that when it came to Jennifer's art my eyes were closed, my ears were deaf, but actually I was frantically preparing to leave for East Germany, making administrative arrangements to access the archives I would need for my research. The reason I had been given permission to do so was that I had promised to engage sensitively in a paper I would write about the realities of everyday life in the GDR. Instead of the usual cold-war stereotypes, I would focus on education, health care and housing for all its citizens, all of which I had discussed with my father before he died.

'If you had ever had to fight a fascist you would put up a wall to keep them out, too.'

When I reminded him the Wall was put up to keep people in, not out, he told me I was the Marie Antoinette of the family and the pearls did not help.

'Take them off, son.'

In his view, freedom of speech and movement were not as important as eliminating inequalities and working for the collective good, but then he could catch the ferry to France any time he liked and no one was going to shoot him from a watchtower in Dover. He turned a blind eye to the Soviet tanks rolling through Prague in 1968 because he obviously thought we were related to Stalin.

'The Soviet Union is the GDR's godfather. Family must look after each other and protect their kin from reactionary adversaries.'

Yeah yeah yeah.

Like Matt looked after his brother when the boys tried to hang me with my tie from the upper deck of the bus. My father disliked what Jennifer described as my 'sublime beauty'; for some reason it offended him. To make it worse, I was physically weaker than my brother and sometimes wore an orange silk tie when I kept our father company in the pub. I once heard him order a pint of bitter for himself and a 'glass of red for the nancy boy'. The barman asked my father if he was okay with Merlot, and handed me the pint of bitter. As a compromise, I laid off the mascara when I attended his talks at Communist Party meetings and replaced the orange silk with a green flat cap made from faux snakeskin. Whenever he was in a bad mood (often) during my early teens, he would shout to Matt, Stalin-style, 'Beat him, beat him,' and Matt, as his accomplice, would punch me down to the floor. Matt was a serious puncher after our mother died. He once split my lip and gave me two intense black eyes, which apparently were more acceptable than my intense blue eyes. It was as if my father's tanks were always parked in the living room of our house in Bethnal Green, ready to roll over my unworthy thirteen-year-old body with their guns raised.

Goodbye, Dad. What else could I say at his funeral?

A lot.

The difference between my father and myself, apart from my education and high cheekbones, was that I believed that people had to be convinced and not coerced. But now that he was dead and couldn't answer back, I missed his certainty.

I was about seven minutes away from the zebra crossing.

Now and then I had to stop to get my breath back. Jennifer's voice kept returning to me. *Can you tell me what actually happened, Saul?*

I resolved to make a note about not forgetting the tin of pineapple. I would write it in capital letters and stick it on the fridge with my 'Zeus the God of the Gods' magnet as soon as I arrived home. In return, Walter Müller had written, he would give me a jar of pickled cucumber, the Emerald of the East, made with fennel and thyme, sugar and vinegar. I wondered if he was aware that the Stasi would be reading his letters? If Stasi informers were known as eyes and ears, it would seem that Jennifer had dumped me because my ears weren't listening and my eyes were closed when it came to her art, and come to think of it, and I did think of it as I picked up speed, I could not recall anything she had told me about her current project, except that I was her muse. Also, I realized that after all the effort to pick up the condoms after the accident, I had not actually used them. They were unopened in the pocket of my torn white jacket.

It was strangely comforting to return to the zebra crossing on Abbey Road. There was no traffic, so it was likely that it had been closed after all.

It occurred to me that when I had first stepped on to that crossing, I had a girlfriend and I was not limping. What came to mind as I sat on the wall outside the EMI studios was the way in which the man who had nearly run me over had touched my hair, as if he were touching a statue or something without a heartbeat.

While I was thinking about this, a woman came up to me waving an unlit cigarette in her hand. She was wearing a blue dress and asked if I had a light. Her short blond hair was so light it was almost silver. Her eyes were the palest green, like glass washed up on a beach. I reached into my pocket and found the metal Zippo lighter I always carried with me, a windproof, old-fashioned, clunky version of the lighter the American military used in the Second World War – later in Vietnam. She grabbed my hand with the lighter in it and peered at the initials carved into the carriage. I explained that it had belonged to my father in the days he used to smoke while he was having his monthly bath. He had died recently and I was taking a small portion of his ashes in a matchbox to bury in communist East Berlin. My hands were shaking as I spoke. I asked her to sit with me for a while, and she did, perching on the wall of the EMI studios, our shoulders touching. I could hear her inhaling and exhaling. Smoke was coming out of her nostrils like the dragon embroidered on Jennifer's kimono. She asked if I was a jittery person.

'Nope.'

'Nervous then?'

A fragment of a poem I did not know I knew came to mind. I spoke it out loud to the woman smoking her cigarette.

'*We are the Dead. Short days ago,*
We lived, felt dawn, saw sunset glow,
Loved and were loved . . .'

She nodded as if I were being normal, which I wasn't.

'It's by John McCrae,' I said. 'He was a Canadian doctor but he signed up as a gunner in the First World War.'

I turned my face towards her and she turned towards me while the wind blew a plastic bag from a supermarket around our feet.

'That's odd,' she said, kicking it away. 'Isn't Wal-Mart American?'

We kissed on the wall like teenagers, her tongue deep in my mouth, my knee wedged between her thighs. When we finally pulled apart, she asked what kind of perfume I was wearing. 'Ylang-ylang,' I said, as she wrote down her telephone number on the palm of my shaking hand. When she walked away, I read the words on the back of her blue dress. It was a uniform. I realized that she was a nurse and that in the song 'Penny Lane' there is a nurse who sells poppies from a tray.

When I arrived home I picked up the telephone and asked a local florist to send a bunch of sunflowers to Hamilton Terrace. I wanted Jennifer to receive them on the day of her graduation show. 'We only have roses': the florist sounded indignant, as if no other kinds of flowers existed in her world. She even seemed offended to hear that although sunflowers were at their peak in August, they were still widely available in September. It was odd to speak to a florist who was terrified of flowers. When I told her that just as sunflowers were coming into bloom, other sorts of flowers were nearing the end of their season, such as poppies, she sounded like she was about to burst into tears.

'We have yellow roses, white roses, red roses, striped roses from China and Burma. Any good? We have a lot of white roses in stock at the moment.'

White roses. Die Weiße Rose – 'the White Rose'. That was the name of the anti-Nazi youth movement in the early 1940s that had started in Munich. I was translating a leaflet for my students, written by the leaders of die Weiße Rose in February 1943.

The Hitler Youth, the SA, the SS have all tried to drug us, to regiment us in the most promising years of our lives.

Perhaps I should order twelve white roses for Jennifer? After all, she was in the most promising years of her life.

No, they had to be sunflowers. They were the only sort of flower she liked to look at in a vase, mostly because of their dark centres, which apparently reminded her of an eclipse, though I'm not sure she had ever seen an eclipse.

I rang another florist and they too did not have sunflowers in stock. Third time lucky I found the sunflowers. This time the florist was a man. He told me he was from Cyprus and that his name was Mike. When he asked me for the message to write on the card, my voice came out strangely shaky and high-pitched. I did not recognize it.

'Sweet Jennifer, good luck for the show, from the careless man who loves you.'

The florist called Mike cleared his throat. 'Sorry, but could you speak in English?'

I couldn't work out what he meant. I repeated the message, along with my name and credit card details. This time my voice was less feeble. There was a pause, then Mike said, 'I don't speak German. I think it's German anyway, but whatever it is you're saying, remember we won the war.'

I could hear him laughing as I kept repeating the message. While he laughed I realized I was thinking my message in English but saying it out loud in German, so I switched to English: 'Sweet Jennifer, good luck for the show, from the careless man who loves you.' After confirming that *careless* was not two words, as in *care less*, we were home and dry. Mike said it was a pleasure doing business with me and that his real name was not Mike. What's more, if he had known I could speak other languages, he would have told me his full name. 'But anyway, take care, Saul.'

That day I had had two people say, 'Take care, Saul.'

When I turned on the shower and washed the blood off my knees, I found myself appalled that Jennifer had not noticed my body was actually grazed and bleeding when we made love. I could smell her ylang-ylang oil on my skin. I am so turned on by ylang-ylang. Afterwards I got on with ironing the shirts I would pack for East Germany.

It took a while to set up the ironing board and fill my vintage iron with water. It was either too hot or too cool but it took my mind off things to point the heavy steel tip at the sleeves, work my way to the cuffs and see the steam rise. I unbuttoned the cuffs and turned them inside out so that I could iron around the buttons. It was crucial not to iron over the buttons, which always leaves a mark. It took me a while to unbutton all the buttons. Frankly, what with the car accident and my first ever offer of marriage being rejected, it felt like I had been beaten up. That was what Stalin most hated, the beatings from his father. I hung up the shirts and stepped on to my balcony. A crowd of sooty ungainly crows were hopping around on the grass of Parliament Hill Fields. One of them suddenly took off and flew towards a bird bath. It was carrying something in its beak and then it dropped it in the bird bath. Maybe it was a mouse, which reminded me that Stalin loved his daughter, Svetlana, as a cat loves a mouse. How did I love Jennifer and how did she love me? I'm not sure she loved me at all. She was definitely the cat and I was the mouse. This made me think that I should have a go at being the cat for a change, but it didn't feel very arousing.

So far, I had kept my part of the deal — to never describe, in words, how amazingly beautiful she was, either to her or to anyone else. Not the colour of her hair or skin or eyes, not the shape of her breasts or lips or nipples, or the length of her thighs or the texture of her pubic hair, or whether her arms were toned or the size of her waist or whether she shaved under her arms or painted her toenails. Apparently, I had no new words with which to describe her, but if I wanted to say, 'She is amazingly beautiful,' that was okay with her because it didn't mean anything. Given that she was always going on about my own sublime beauty, I wondered if it meant anything. To her. She was making it mean something in her photographs, but she said these weren't really about me, it was the whole composition that was important and I was just one part of it. Why had she outlined my lips in red felt-tip in that photograph above her bed? I knew how much she loved to kiss me, so why did she write, *DON'T KISS ME*? It was as if she thought that having sex made her vulnerable and gave me too much power. Jennifer did not want to give me that sort of power, so I just had to busk it with her. She was quite interested in a male student at her art school called Otto. He had blue hair and was her age. Even if she believed that he was destined to become the new most famous artist in the world, I knew that black was the colour of her true love's hair.

4

I unlocked the postbox in the lobby of my apartment block to see if the Abbey Road photographs had arrived. These would be my gift to Luna Müller, the younger sister of my translator, Walter Müller. When I'd put the key into the lock, it had felt slightly loose, as if the screws had been gouged out and then hastily screwed back again. Yet when I'd looked at the postboxes for the other tenants, I could see they were also in a state of disrepair. The wood on all of them was chipped. Most of the brass locks, which were made in the 1930s, were missing screws. It had been more difficult than usual to align the key with the hole. The landlord raised our rents every year but did nothing to repair the building, which was more or less falling down. The old lady from upstairs, Mrs Stechler, stepped out of the lift and hobbled into the lobby, her gloved hands gripping the steel tube of her Zimmer. She seemed startled to find me on my knees, staring at the locks on all the postboxes. She wore a fur coat and started complaining about her arthritis, how the wet weather inflamed it and made her even more lame. 'Rain is bad news for my bones,' she said in her gloomy, deep voice. I glanced through the glass doors of the lobby. The sun was shining. The grass in the communal gardens was still yellow from the heatwave that summer. The autumn leaves were not wet.

'Something wrong, Saul?'

'No.'

'I wanted to ask about your surname,' she said.

'What about it?'

'On your postbox you have the name Saul Adler.'

'Yes.'

'Adler is a Jewish name.'

'So?'

She waited for me to say more and I did say more.

'Saul is a Jewish name, too. All right with you?'

Her mouth hung open as if she were searching for a bigger hole to breathe through. It would seem that my name was the spectre haunting Mrs Stechler.

I stood up because it was too abject talking to her on my knees. After a while, I asked if she could tell me where to buy a tin of pineapple.

'Everywhere. Every shop has a tin of pineapple. Even the corner shop. Do you want slices or chunks? Syrup or juice?'

She stared at me through her thick spectacles, as if I were a thief intent on robbing all the postboxes in the building. I had found an envelope in my postbox and was curious to open it but didn't want her to watch me. She told me she was going to buy a slice of poppy-seed cake at the new Polish shop, and while she was at it she needed to find something to remove the stain on her turtle-green sofa. I was thinking about turtles and what kind of green represented them in the upholstery business when she started to complain again about the pain in her joints and the weather. I could not recall a Polish shop in the street she had named. There was a butcher's shop and a newsagent, and a hair salon that mostly catered to pensioners like herself, but nothing that resembled a Polish shop, unless the Bengali newsagent had started to sell Eastern European pastries. I was distracted because I had now opened the envelope and was staring at the photos, three of them, in black and white.

There I was, walking barefoot on the zebra crossing in my white suit with the flared trousers, my hands in the pockets of the white jacket. There was a note from Jennifer:

By the way, it's not John Lennon who walked barefoot. That was Paul. JL wore white shoes. Managed to get you in mid-stride like the original, thanks to my trusty stepladder.

I did not remember taking off my shoes, but it was true, I was barefoot in the photograph. When I looked up, I saw that Mrs Stechler had left her Zimmer in the lobby, tucked behind the porter's desk. Through the glass doors I could see her in her fur coat, walking at a brisk pace in the direction of the bus stop. Wasn't she supposed to be crippled with arthritis?

I put the photographs back in my postbox, locked it and walked to my nearest supermarket to buy the tin of pineapple for Walter Müller. What would Jennifer be doing today? Probably sorting out her air ticket to America. Obviously, she'd be in the dark room at college, preparing for her graduation show, and later, much later, she would be lazing in the sauna with Saanvi and Claudia, talking about infinity and how a manically depressed mathematician called Georg Cantor found a way of notating infinite numbers. Meanwhile, I was trying to figure out whether to buy tinned pineapple in rings or chunks, in syrup or juice. In the end I bought two bananas, a baguette, a slice of steak, and then found myself lingering at the cheese counter. I began to feel some sympathy with the florist who only sold roses. If there was an infinity of roses to choose from, it was the same with cheese. Shropshire Blue, Stilton, Farmhouse Cheddar, Lancashire, Red Leicester, Gouda, Emmental.

I asked the male assistant to scoop me up a large wedge of oozing Brie. It dripped from his knife. He had gentle hands.

The sky was grey and so was the pavement. It had started to rain. A man in an African robe was struggling with a broken umbrella while the rain splashed over his sandals. I stopped for a glass of tea and a baklava pastry at a Turkish café. The pastry was sticky with honey. I asked for a napkin but the woman serving me did not seem to hear my request. She walked towards a young girl, about seven years old, reading a book at a table nearby, and whispered something in her ear. I thought she was asking the child to fetch me a napkin but she was adjusting one of the red ribbons in her daughter's plaited hair.

'It's like this, Saul Adler: the main subject is not always you.'

It's like this, Jennifer Moreau: you have made me the main subject.

5

Something was going on in my apartment block. People were running out of the building in a panic. The engineer who lived on the third floor was shouting about a fire. I couldn't smell anything burning. There was a rumour that the firefighters were on strike, although it had not been officially announced. The landlord had advised us all to keep a bucket of sand at the ready just in case, and also to unplug all unnecessary electrical devices except for the fridge. Mrs Stechler came back with what she said was the poppy-seed cake, but I could see through the plastic bag she was holding in her gloved hands, and it looked like chunks of bloody chopped meat. When she collected her Zimmer from the lobby, she told me she thought she might have left her toaster plugged in, and come to think of it, she wasn't sure if she had switched off her electric heater. Why would she have her electric heater on in September? I volunteered to run up to her apartment and check. There was a debate amongst the other tenants gathered outside the building about whether this was wise. It was decided that if there was a fire, I should not take the risk, but when I insisted, they advised me to at least avoid the lift.

'He wants to die, so let him.' Mrs Stechler actually smiled as she handed over her door keys. It was the first time I had ever seen her cheerful.

I did not run up the five flights of stairs; I walked slowly because I was still limping from the fall on the Abbey Road crossing. There was no sign of smoke when I opened her door with the keys. Everything was turned off in her flat. A heavy black telephone was positioned in the middle of the carpet. That was a strange place to keep a phone, particularly if she had arthritis and couldn't easily lower herself to the floor. I tracked the cord and saw it was plugged into the wall socket behind the television. I made my hand into a fist and started tapping it against the wall. If I was looking for something, I wasn't sure what I wanted to find. Was the wall hollow or was it solid? Is that what I wanted to know? I tapped again. It was as if this action made me feel important, which made me wonder if I felt unimportant the rest of the time. Did the Stasi feel more important when they were tapping walls with their fists? The telephone rang and I picked up the receiver.

'Hello. Mrs Stechler's phone.'

'Who is this?'

'My name is Saul. I'm a neighbour.'

'It's Isaac.'

A pain shot through my chest.

'Mrs Stechler is not in. Can I take a message?'

'Saul who?'

The words *Saul who?* filled me with terror and dread and regret.

All the same, I made an effort to speak clearly and softly into the phone.

'Saul Adler.'

I could barely speak at all.

I realized that I was heartbroken. The Wal-Mart carrier bag that had flown in with the wind on Abbey Road was connected to America in another time, and the name Isaac was connected to America, too.

The line went dead.

Someone was breathing close to me.

I turned around and looked straight into the startled eyes of an animal. A black poodle had jumped on to the arm of the sofa. Its eyes were wet and it was whimpering. Leaseholders and tenants are not supposed to keep animals in the flats. I'd had no idea Mrs Stechler had a dog. Her purchase of raw meat instead of poppy-seed cake now made sense.

I sat on the sofa and held the poodle in my arms. The telephone started to ring again. As I stroked the dog's warm head, I became calmer. Our breathing had somehow synchronized; we were breathing together as we waited for the phone to stop ringing. It was very tranquil to hold the dog in my arms and to breathe in time with it.

I was hungry. Ravenous. Maybe I had forgotten to eat since the near collision on Abbey Road. Sitting on the turtle-green sofa in what might be an emergency (the suspected fire) made me think of my friend Jack, who had told me he never wanted children. Jack thought that parents were aliens who spoke in weird voices to their children, and anyway, he wanted to be the centre of attention, especially the sexual attention of his lovers. No way did he want that attention stolen from him by the needs of a child or the now-endless needs of the alien parent.

I had heartily agreed with him. Jack was ten years older than me but looked younger than his thirty-eight years. He wore stylish linen jackets with black teenage sneakers, which I had always thought was a good look.

I wasn't so sure I thought so the day we were eating moules frites in a French bistro in West London. I was aware over that lunch that we regarded ourselves as cultured, sophisticated, good-looking men, a cut above the exhausted fathers who probably had not had sex for a long time. Or not with their exhausted partners anyway.

Yet, even then, I did not totally believe myself as I agreed with Jack. Although he was droll and amusing, he was somehow lacking in feeling. I said this out loud to the dog who was now asleep on my lap.

'He was somehow lacking in feeling.'

When Jack looked over at my plate of moules, he noticed I had left some of them uneaten. He asked if he could polish them off for me, as if he were doing me a great favour. I pushed my bowl in his direction, watching him guzzle everything, slurping the shells and chewing very fast – he thought this slurping of my leftovers made him very lovable. Which was odd. (I said this out loud again to the poodle: 'It was odd.') I was enjoying reminiscing about Jack with a decorative, illegal dog on my lap. If there was a fire after all, perhaps I should save its life? It was true that I could smell something acrid, bitter, but was it smoke?

I had more thoughts on handsome Jack to gather in.

I took the dog's paw in my hand and squeezed it. After Jack had eaten my moules, he turned his attention to the bill that had now arrived on a saucer. He glanced at it and, instead of us splitting the cost equally, he insisted that as I had ordered extra bread and they had charged us for it, I should cover the cost, despite him participating in the extra bread. At the same time, he was eyeing a portion of lemon tart the man sitting solo at the table next to us had left unfinished on his plate. Jack wanted to reach over and gobble up that, too. When he glanced conspiratorially at me, I asked myself why he was so unlovable. I think this question was on my mind when I was tapping the wall with my fist. The answer was obviously because Jack himself was unloving. I had asked the wall a question and, in its way, it had answered. I was suddenly worried that Jennifer might think that I was unloving. Jack was supposed to be playing tennis after our meal. He told me he had taken a few extra lessons from a coach to perfect his serve for this particular match. I couldn't work out why he would gobble a large lunch before a tennis game, but he was very thin. I supposed that he himself was the child he so deplored. A child that needed feeding up.

In the meantime it was possible that while I was sitting on the sofa, stroking an illegal dog, the apartment block was in flames. I stood up and dropped the black poodle to the floor. It made an indignant sound as I picked up the paper bag with the Brie in it and slammed the front door. Again, I limped down the stairs, but I could not smell smoke.

Everyone was huddled outside the block, pointing at various windows. They were all relieved to know that Mrs Stechler had not left the heater on. I told her that someone had called for her.

She took off her thick spectacles and looked confused.

'I don't think so. My phone has been cut off.'

She started to blow on her spectacle lenses and then scooped up the hem of her dress and wiped her eyes.

'By the way,' she said, 'I am Jewish, too. I was born in Kraków.'

The engineer tapped my shoulder.

'Thank you for doing the health-and-safety check, Mr Adler,' he said sincerely. 'It has put our minds at rest.'

I wondered why Mrs Stechler was wearing gloves and what kind of spectre lay beneath them, but I didn't want to think about that so I ran across the road and called Jennifer from the payphone on the corner.

'How are you, Jennifer?'

'Why are you calling me?'

'Because the firefighters are on strike.'

'Who says the firefighters are on strike? First I've heard of it.'

I was holding the bag with the melting Brie in my hand. Jennifer was speaking in a friendly, casual sort of way, as if she had not turned down my offer of marriage, and, after making use of my body, had not more or less turfed me out of her bed, still bruised and bleeding from the accident.

'The photographs came out well didn't they?' She started to talk about light and shadow and the angle from which she had taken the photos and how in the original photograph of the real Beatles, for the album *Abbey Road*, there had been an American tourist standing under a tree who just happened to be there at the time. I was peering at the paper bag with the wedge of Brie melting inside it. There seemed to be some kind of message written on the right-hand corner of the bag.

'Are you okay, Saul?'

33

The shop assistant with the gentle hands had written the price of the cheese in biro and underlined it twice.

'No, I am not okay, not at all.'

'It's like this, Saul Adler: fuck off.'

'It's like this, Jennifer Moreau: that's exactly what I'm going to do.'

That night, when I packed my bag for East Berlin, I realized I had forgotten to buy the tin of pineapple.

6

East Berlin, September 1988

I spent a lot of time laughing with Walter Müller. It was a relief to hang out with someone whose life was not about material gain. Walter was a master linguist. He taught Eastern European languages to East Germans who were heading off to work in other socialist countries, and he was fluent in the English language as well. I liked him as soon as I saw him waiting for me at Friedrichstraße station. He was standing at the end of the platform, holding up a piece of cardboard with my name written on it. He was about thirty, with shoulder-length mousy hair, pale blue eyes, tall, broad shoulders. Muscular. There was a kind of energy in his body, a vitality that was relaxed but exciting. I told him about the nightmare train journey to the British airport and how the train had run out of fuel and how I'd had to wait for a replacement bus. Walter Müller shook his head in a vaguely mocking way to express the depth of his sympathy. Obviously, in his view, I was paddling in the shallow end of life's problems.

'That is very bad mismanagement of your country's transport system.'

He steered me out of Friedrichstraße and asked if I wished to walk to his mother's apartment or would prefer to take a tram. I agreed that we should walk. His English was formal, slightly uptight, unlike the confidence and zip in his body.

'This is our city on the Spree,' he said, waving his hands in the direction of the river. We walked along the grey waters of the Spree as we made our way past the Berliner Ensemble theatre, founded by Brecht, who had spent the Nazi years in exile. He had lived in at least four countries. I named them for Walter.

'Sweden, Finland, Denmark, eventually America.'

'Oh yes, Brecht,' Walter said. 'Did you know that Bruce Springsteen gave a concert here in July? He played for three hours.' He corrected himself. 'No. Four hours.'

I knew that Brecht had been regarded with suspicion by the authorities because he had chosen to live in America and not the Soviet Union. All the same, he had returned to East Germany to write his plays, hoping to play a part in building a new socialist state. It seemed that I was more interested in Brecht than my translator, so I did not tell him that I knew all the words to *The Threepenny Opera* ('an opera for beggars') and often sang 'Surabaya Johnny' in the bath. I looked down at two white swans swimming side by side on the Spree.

'Swans like to live together,' I said. 'They establish strong bonds with each other.'

Walter tried to look interested. 'Thank you for the information.' His voice was serious but his eyes were laughing.

Walter told me he had just returned from Prague, where he had been translating from Czech into German for comrades who had signed up for an engineering course. When I thanked him for meeting me at the station, given that he had just returned from his own travelling, he laughed. 'This walk with you is my good fortune. I can do something purposeful, like taking you for a beer.' A fly was buzzing around his lips. He waved it away and then stamped his boot on the cobblestones to elicit extra fear.

'Magic.' He laughed, stamping his boot again.

'Magic,' I repeated. I wasn't sure what was going on or why he was laughing.

'Whatever you do,' he said, 'when you write your report on our republic, don't say everything was grey and crumbling except for the colourful interruption of red flags positioned on buildings.'

'Absolutely not.' I looked into his pale blue eyes with my intense blue eyes. 'I will note there are flies. And that many of the tram drivers are female.' I did not yet know him well enough to tell him I had become used to being censored because Jennifer had forbidden me from describing her in my own old words.

We continued our convivial conversation. Walter walked briskly in his heavy winter coat while I tried to keep up in my light jacket. He told me how much he liked the name of a certain cake in Prague. It was called a 'little coffin' and was mostly made from cream. I reckoned he was talking about an eclair.

He asked if I knew the work of the Czech artist Eva Švankmajerová. I did not. He admired a sentence she had written; he would try and translate it for me now. He shut his eyes – 'Here goes' – and frowned for a long time as he tried to gather the words across three languages, Czech, German, English, then he opened his eyes, punched my arm and shook back his hair. 'It's not possible to translate.' What he really liked to do in Prague was to knock back a shot of slivovitz, 'a very old one, from Moravia'. Soon he would introduce me to the university director, who was likely to offer me a good-quality schnapps.

After a while he asked why I was limping. I told him in German about the near accident on Abbey Road and he said in English, 'So are we speaking German or English to each other?'

'Well, maybe we can do fifty–fifty,' I said in German.

'How come you speak fluent German?' he asked in English.

'My mother was born in Heidelberg.'

'So you are half German?'

'She came to Britain when she was eight.'

'Did she speak German at home?'

'Never.'

This time he did not thank me for the information.

When I continued to limp, he bluntly asked if I was lame.

'I am not lame. I've just got a bruised hip.'

I said this loudly and with feeling. I did not want to seem pathetic to Walter Müller. No. Not at all. I wanted to seem something else, but the truth was that I had a pain in my stomach. It felt as if something were being removed from my guts with a knife.

He offered to carry my bag. I refused but he took it anyway, slinging it over his shoulder as we walked down a cobblestoned road called Marienstraße. After a while he pointed to the hospital where his sister worked as a nurse. 'The doctors are very good,' he said, 'but it's best not to have to stay the night there. She could arrange an X-ray for you if you like?'

'No!' I thumped his shoulder so hard he began to laugh.

'You're stronger than you look.'

I don't think he meant it because he pushed me away when I tried to get my bag back from him.

A tram was clanking by in the distance.

'Sit down, Saul.' Walter pointed to a stone step at the entrance of one of the apartment blocks.

I sat down on the step as instructed. He sat next to me, my bag shoved between his knees. Everything was peaceful and calm. I noticed that Walter had now put on a pair of spectacles and was reading his newspaper. The sky had darkened and his left arm was resting across my shoulders. I felt happy. Inexplicably happy. It was like the moment I'd sat on Mrs Stechler's sofa with the illegal poodle on my lap. We sat like that for a long time.

After a while, he folded his newspaper and patted my shoulder.

'Tell me about your accident.'

I began to speak. I heard myself say things I did not know I thought. I told Walter that what really worried me on Abbey Road was that my mother had died in a car crash when I was twelve. Somehow, irrationally, I thought Wolfgang – that was the name of the driver, I told him – might have been the same person who had killed her.

'That is an understandable fear,' Walter said.

I told him how my hands had started to shake when I returned to the site of the accident and how I sat on the wall with the woman who had asked me to light her cigarette. The shaking, I told him, was to do with the memory of the first seconds of hearing the news that my mother had died and would never be coming home. And then a second memory of realizing that this meant I was to live with my father and brother without my mother, who had used her body like a human wall to protect me from them.

'You needed protecting from your father and brother?'

'Yes. They were big men. They would have liked you.'

He shook his head and laughed. 'I don't think so.'

'Walter,' I said, 'where is the Wall? I can't see it.'

'It is everywhere.'

I told him that my mother's fatal accident and my minor accident had become blurred in my mind and how I was still insatiably angry with the driver who had run her over. I regarded him as her assassin. Time passing had not made my mother's death less vivid. All the same, I had not really been paying attention when I crossed the road.

'Ah, yes.' Walter folded his newspaper, first in half, and then again. As I watched his fingers smooth out the corners, I noticed they were covered with grey ink from the newspaper. Random words were smudged like ash on his fingertips. I could hear the sound of typing in my head. The keys hammering a page. It was as if I were informing on myself. *Herr Adler is a careless man*. But those were not the words Walter was saying to me now.

'Perhaps you needed to repeat it or something?'

'Repeat what?'

'History.'

He leaned forward and asked if he could help tie my left shoelace. It had come undone on our walk. My humiliation was unending. He was kind and unjudging, as strangers sometimes can be, usually because history has not got in the way. I stood up and began to walk on without him. I had no idea where I was heading but I did not want him to see my tears. I had just arrived and here he was, carrying my bag, tying my shoelaces, and now I was weeping. When he caught up with me he had taken off his spectacles. There was a welt on the bridge of his nose where the plastic had pressed into his skin.

'Hey, Saul, wait for me.'

He was standing next to a woman carrying a wooden box. It turned out to be full of small cauliflowers. Walter spoke to her in a dialect I did not understand. I think he was giving me time to discreetly wipe my eyes. The problem was that my eyes would not dry up. I'd wipe them and then more tears would pelt down. I was embarrassed beyond measure to have brought such a large portion of my own sorrow to the GDR. Yes, it was such a big helping. I needed my friend Jack, who finished off everyone's food, to take some of it from me. Jack's ungenerous nature was the opposite of Walter's, though Walter was no less sophisticated. He was certainly less stylish and less aggressive. I began to understand more of what he was saying to the woman holding the box. He was talking about cherries. Something about the cherry tree on the allotment of his family's dacha. He had also planted cauliflowers but they had not taken. All of them were blighted. She looked into the middle distance, somewhere just above my head, but I knew she was looking at me.

I waved to her. She did not respond, her face a façade of stone. I suddenly understood that it might be dangerous for her to make contact with Westerners. Someone would report her for waving back at me. I could see no beggars or junkies or pimps or thieves or anyone sleeping on the streets. Yet the expression in her eyes stayed with me, as did her red lips. Would I prefer to have my wallet stolen if it meant I felt free to greet a stranger without fear? She and Walter seemed to know each other because he kissed her cheek and she gave him a cauliflower. Walter reached into his pocket and took out a red string bag. He dropped the cauliflower into the bag and slung it over his shoulder.

'Quite good luck,' he shouted to me.

We continued walking. It was easier now that the pain in my stomach had faded. I asked him about his allotment. He told me he was looking into keeping bees and invited me to spend a weekend in the dacha on the outskirts of the city so I could see it for myself.

'I would like that very much, thank you.' Apparently, we were still a long way from his mother's apartment. I asked him why his sister was called Luna.

'The moon is a source of light. And Luna is my mother's source of light. Her first daughter did not survive.'

To hear those words touched a pain that was deep inside me, along with all the other pains. Like a pond of black water. Lit by the moon.

When I wasn't limping, I was crying. It was a terrible start.

'Not long to the pub,' Walter said, 'but first I must drop off the cauliflower.' He led me through the inner courtyard of an old stone building and told me to wait by the stairwell.

Once again, I sat on the steps. This time I tied my own shoelaces.

The walls of the apartment block were gouged with bullet holes from the last war. My father would have got straight to work on plastering the walls of the GDR. I found myself preoccupied with Walter's description of the blighted cherry tree that grew in the garden of his dacha. Although I was sitting on a stone step in East Berlin, I was receiving images from somewhere else. They were all in black and white, like Jennifer's photographs. A clapboard house on Cape Cod, America. The house was built from pine and cedar. Inside it was a large fireplace. The windows were hung with wooden shutters. Jennifer was somewhere in that house and her hair had turned white.

I could hear the cries of gulls from the Cape Cod seashore and the banks of the Spree in East Berlin.

When Walter came down the stairs he was holding a tiny toy train carved from wood.

'I have to mend it.' He slipped the train into the pocket of his coat. 'The glue is at my mother's place.'

41

He was trying to explain something complicated to me in German. It seemed to be about how he did not live with his mother and sister. I didn't understand and asked if we could speak seventy per cent English instead of fifty until I found my feet.

I placed the palm of my hand on his chest, leaning into him while I got my breath back from the shock of glimpsing that wooden train. One of its wheels, painted red, poked out of Walter's coat pocket. I had seen that train before, or dreamed it, or even buried it, and here it was, returning like a spectre to torment me.

'You all right, Saul?'

'Most definitely,' I replied.

Walter suggested we take a tram to the pub.

7

The flat that I was to share with Walter's mother and his sister Luna was surprisingly spacious. Three of the walls in the living room were covered in orange swirling wallpaper. Walter told me that in winter this room was heated with brown coal. He showed me the ceramic-tiled coal oven. It smelled acrid, nothing like sooty black coal, but that was apparently because the brown coal came in briquettes. It was one of the few national resources in the GDR and was heavily mined, so whole regions had been stripped bare. The coal man arrived early in the morning carrying bags of these heavy briquettes to the court-yard. It was Luna's job to clean out the ashes and she always complained like a spoilt czarina, but it was not a big job. Right now, his sister would be queuing for a very rare delivery of bananas after work. She was crazy for fruit. Any sort of fruit except apples.

'I never get stressed about bananas.' Walter sounded quite stressed. 'I don't need to eat bananas when they became available. But I do like the oranges when they arrive from Cuba.'

I looked around the living room while he spoke. We were getting nearer the subject of pineapple and I suppose I was searching for somewhere to hide. The telephone that was placed in the middle of the table looked like Mrs Stechler's phone in London. A tray positioned near it was set with a tall white teapot, two china cups and saucers stacked next to it. A mirror framed in heavy dark wood hung on the wall, and oddly, next to it, a calendar from 1977, a pin-up of a woman posing in a gold leopard-spotted bikini with matching gold fingernails. A fake yellow rose was pinned to the left side of her hair. After talking about fruit for a while, Walter showed me my bedroom. A chaste single bed was pushed against the wall. It was made up with two blankets and one small pillow, a blue towel folded neatly on the covers. He told me his mother would be home soon to cook something, but usually he did all the cooking in the family. Someone was knocking on the front door. First a loud knock, then three light taps.

It turned out to be a colleague of Walter's from the university. His name was Rainer and he had strapped an acoustic guitar across his khaki jacket. Rainer was dressed in hippyish clothes and held some sort of administrative post, helping with photocopying and seminar-room bookings. He was dreamy and quiet in his khaki jacket and purple flares. They were too long for him so he'd turned up the ends. Rainer told me he liked to read the American beat poets but had to smuggle their books into the GDR. Walter asked after his sister, who had been unwell. 'Oh, she's still angry.' He strummed a few chords on his guitar and explained how his sister was part of a youth brigade who had recently helped clean up the grounds of an apartment block that was run-down. She had been up on the roof doing small repairs; it had been a hot summer so she had worn shorts and a bikini top. Her friend who was also part of the youth brigade had taken a photograph of her, but her camera had been confiscated and the film exposed by the authorities so now her mother had said she couldn't see her girl-friend any more. Earlier, when Walter and I were having a few beers in the pub, he had told me how he had also been part of a youth group in his teens and the point of it was to create solidarity between young people who felt materially inferior to the West. He thought that was a good thing, but he didn't like wearing the uniform.

He was listening to Rainer, unsmiling and stern. After a while he told him he doubted the camera would have been confiscated and the film exposed if there was nothing offensive on it. He did not sound like himself. I remembered Jennifer telling me there was a spectre inside every photograph she developed in the dark room. Rainer was laughing as he strummed his battered guitar. 'Yeah, it's true that we have many enemies trying to perpetrate sabotage wherever they can.' Rainer didn't sound like himself either, but as I hardly knew him, or Walter, how would I know that? Perhaps there was a listening device hidden behind the big mirror on the wall.

All the same, Rainer was easy company. He told me he was part of a church discussion group promoting peace and a more relaxed way of living. In his view, if your government is violent to its people at home but preaches peace abroad, something is not right. Even though it was likely his group was under surveillance because there were quite a few punks and young green activists who wanted another system, including the priest himself, all they did was play guitar and sing and talk.

'What did you do today? Did Walter take you for a beer?'

'We bought a cauliflower,' Walter replied.

'Cool.' Rainer was smiling again. His teeth were very straight and white and not at all British – or East German, for that matter.

When I looked at Walter he wasn't smiling. Perhaps he was tired from having to carry my bag and tie my shoelaces and walk at a child's pace and pretend not to notice I was crying. After a while Rainer said he had to go, but to let him know if I needed any help with my research. I told him that actually I needed to photocopy some notes I was making for a lecture I was writing.

'No problem.' He stood up and fiddled with the straps on his guitar while I sorted out my crumpled illegible notes.

Of course, I didn't give him my notes on the psychology of male tyrants. On how Stalin's father was a drunk who beat his son viciously, so he had a reason never to become the underdog again. No, I gave Rainer a comprehensive list of all Stalin's achievements and a timeline. 'I'll have them ready for you on Monday.' He flicked me a V sign, the one that means peace, and encouraged me to get drunk.

*

A few minutes after he left, the mirror that was hanging on the orange wall fell down. The sound of it hitting the floor made me jump. The last time I had seen a shattered mirror was on the Abbey Road crossing. The wing mirror of the car, Wolfgang's car, had exploded into a heap of reflective shards. Walter and I walked to the mirror and noted that it was intact. It had not even cracked. I was gazing at the wallpaper to see if there was a listening device underneath it but the surface looked flat and neatly papered. We each held a side of the mirror and hung it up again. When it was firmly attached to the rusty nail on the wall, I glanced at Walter in the mirror. His eyes were staring into my eyes. He was not making small talk with his eyes. And then he looked away. I could see him in the mirror looking elsewhere and I thought about the way Stalin had eradicated the past by deleting from the historical record whatever he found inconvenient. Yet I knew that look was a historical record of Walter's desire. There was no way it could be deleted.

His eyes were on me all the time.

He watched me as I reached into the grey canvas sling bag that was usually crammed with the books I carried to my lectures. I took out a matchbox, opened it and showed him the spoonful of my father's ashes inside. Walter looked baffled. I explained that my father, who had been a communist since he was fourteen, had recently died and that I wanted to bury part of him in the soil of East Germany. He had admired the GDR for attempting to make a society that was different from its fascist predecessors and so I needed to find a place to bury his ashes.

Walter was examining the little wooden train. One of its red wheels had snapped off. He seemed disappointed and strained. I realized he must have thought I was reaching into my bag for the tin of pineapple I had promised to bring with me from London. When I made that journey to my local supermarket, still shocked from the accident, I had gazed for a long time at the rows of tinned fruit, every sort of fruit and every variety of tinned pineapple. Yet, somehow, I had been distracted and had moved on to the cheese counter. Walter was now looking at the wallpaper, the ceiling, the floor, anything but the matchbox in my hands.

'I apologize, Walter. I forgot the pineapple.'

I explained how I was in a frantic rush when I left Britain. Meetings at the university, marking student dissertations, sorting out last-minute visa problems. I thought it best not to mention the abundance of the cheese counter, where I had become distracted by the gentle hands of the man showing me the wedge of ripe Brie. Walter glanced at the matchbox of grey ash on the table and shook his head. To swap the ashes of a corpse for a tin of pineapple was an affront, an insult. How had I forgotten the humble tin of pineapple he had requested? I could feel myself blushing. It was as if my whole body were on fire, which made me think of the fire in my apartment block when I returned from the supermarket without the tin of pineapple. I wondered if the fire that never happened was my own shame.

'It's okay,' he said. 'It happens.'

I took out a wad of West German marks and laid them on the table. I was feeling very uncomfortable.

'We can get the pineapple from the Intershop.'

'You're not supposed to have West marks here, put them away.'

I was surprised at how authoritarian he sounded. That is to say, he was assuming an authority that I had not initially thought he possessed, or even wanted to possess. He was ventriloquizing the voice of the state and he sounded like my father.

I suppose I wanted to prove myself to him as something more than a decadent bourgeois who had forgotten to bring a tin of pineapple to my hosts. I told him how my father had been a builder, a plasterer, and how he used to mix horsehair into the plaster to stop it from cracking. He called the tool to stack plaster, the flat square wooden board with a handle attached to the middle, 'the hawk'.

He worked with his hawk and his trowel all his life. Sometimes when he did an exterior job he would add marble dust to the plaster. My father's oldest brother was a blacksmith, making not just horse-shoes but parts for the railways and shipyards. And my brother was an electrician. I was the first person in my family to go to university.

'Oh yes. Good for you.'

He put on a Bruce Springsteen record and left the room. I saw him dancing around in the kitchen while he filled a pot with water. I quickly put the matchbox back in my bag. Even the backs of my hands were blushing. I made my scarlet right hand into a fist and started tapping it against the wall of the apartment. The tapping made me feel less fragile, as if I were searching for something that I alone knew was there. Walter watched me from the kitchen. He was laughing while he danced. At one point he shouted, 'Found anything yet?' When he came out carrying two small cups, he glanced at the place on my neck where the buttons were undone. I was still burning up with blush.

'My mother has nearly run out of coffee but she's got a good supply of sugar so this is mostly sugar and the rest is chicory.'

We sat down on two hard chairs, facing each other.

He leaned forward and, with his little finger, touched the corner of my eye. A speck of plaster from the wall had lodged itself near my eyelid.

And then he raised his cup.

'To meeting you, Saul, here in East Berlin in 1988.'

I sipped the coffee that didn't taste of coffee, but it was sweet and hot, like he said.

'You know, Walter, I don't think that's the right date.'

'So, when are you living?'

'Further on.'

The sun was setting over the bullet-wounded buildings.

I leaned forward and whispered in Walter's ear, like a lover,

'Germany East and West will be one. There will be a revolution. With the exception of Romania there will be no blood shed on the streets.'

'And what will be the motivation for these revolutions?' He was whispering too, his lips near my ear.

'In East Germany the motivation is not just for the better economic life over the other side of the Wall. Yes, I know you are frustrated with the authoritarian regime, but that is not the motivation either. The economy of the Soviet Union will be on the brink of collapse. Soviet communism is going to fall. General Secretary Gorbachev is the man who will end the cold war.'

Our knees touched.

'Listen to me, Walter. It will be possible for citizens of the GDR to cross the border whenever they please.'

He started to cough.

I did not know if the future I had outlined had stuck like a bone in Walter's throat or if he was just overwhelmed.

He stood up, walked to the kitchen and splashed cold water over his face.

When he returned, Walter was pacing the room, his arms folded against his chest. His face was shockingly pale.

I reached over and touched the buckle of his belt. I could hear a voice in my head like the loudspeaker of a train announcing 'Attention', but it was too late. My right hand reached for the ends of his long hair, which smelled of brown coal. He pushed me away. It was insulting but also flirtatious, a display of his physical strength, perhaps a threat.

The door opened and a woman walked in carrying a bag of flour.

'Hallo.' She slammed the flour on the table.

'My name is Ursula. I am Walter's mother. It's so warm today my sister tells me the youngsters are swimming in the fountain in Leipzig.'

Walter's heavy coat was draped over the back of a chair. Perhaps he did not possess clothes for the end of summer when it was still warm. I smelled the heady scent of roses. Ursula was wearing a strong, sweet perfume.

'Good evening. I'm Saul Adler.'

'I know. Who else would you be?'

She shook my hand. Her hair was dyed a deep red. It was fading at the roots.

'I'm stocking up on flour,' she said in English, 'because I'm going to bake Luna a pineapple cake.'

Her hand lingered in my hand.

'It's her birthday next week and she says she would have our wall built one metre higher for just one piece of pineapple.'

8

The librarian in charge of the archive at the university seemed to have a very low opinion of me. I spoke either too loudly or too softly or too fast or not fast enough. She did not seem to know much about the various newspapers and journals I needed to access for my research. When I asked to speak to another member of staff, she told me, in a voice that resembled two hundred kilometres of barbed wire, that I was being disrespectful.

The textbooks I was given by the secretary to the director of the university were all propaganda, so were the newspapers and TV programmes, but none of it was unfamiliar to me. I had heard it all before from my father. I knew the Stasi would be interested in my presence at the university but not fascinated. After all, I was not a spy or here to encourage anyone to flee the country. All the same, it was likely there would be an invisible eye and ear somewhere nearby. My own eyes and ears had become hyper-alert, but so far, apart from the librarian, I had not seen anyone watching me. Yet the fact that I was searching for someone who might be there, as if their absence were more threatening than their presence, as if lack of surveillance were more peculiar than constant surveillance, reminded me of how I felt after my father died. It was hard to believe he was no longer here to find fault with all I said and did and to punish me for my flaws. I think I was paranoid way before I arrived in East Berlin.

I began to regard my own eyes and ears as advanced surveillance technologies.

With the exception of the librarian, most of the staff were helpful and welcoming. I was content to spend most of the days researching the inspiring youth movement that had begun in the Rhineland as an alternative to the quasi-military culture of the Hitler Youth, of which membership was compulsory after 1936. Endearingly, they'd named their group the Edelweiss Pirates. Most cities in western Germany had had some kind of Pirates group, even if they hadn't got together under that name. Their ages ranged from twelve to eighteen, they wore bohemian checked shirts, sang parodies of the Hitler Youth anthem and were keen on the jazz and blues coming through from France. The boys grew their hair long to protest against the mindset of their fathers. I would have been happy to lend them my orange silk tie and faux-snakeskin cap. They were all the more impressive because most of the young Pirates had a school education that was under Nazi control. It took some doing to resist their minds being invaded before Poland was invaded.

Our song is freedom, love and life,
We're the Pirates of the Edelweiss

Their parents would have read newspapers such as *Der Stürmer*, crammed with ugly cartoon caricatures of Jews. On the way to school they might have passed shops that sold instruments to measure the difference in size between Aryan and non-Aryan skulls. The young Pirates attempted to make all this go away for a few hours when they met together. My subject was cultural resistance to Nazism, yet the advice of scientists, doctors, academics and lawyers had been enthusiastically given to the Nazi racial programme. Genocide offered opportunities to acquire wealth: abandoned factories, shops, family properties and furniture. Seventy-two trainloads of gold were sent to Berlin from Auschwitz. The gold had been gouged out of the teeth of men and women who would never see their home again. Fascism, working hand in hand with nationalism, had industrialized mass murder, organized the transportation of cheap poison gases and recruited euthanasia operatives.

I had found a blue eyeliner pencil in one of my pockets. It was called Ocean Spray and had been given to me by Jennifer for my last birthday. I usually wore a suit and tie to the library, hoping to signify I was a serious scholar with thoughts that were in total sync with a regime ideologically policed by old men in suits. Yes, the regime and I could sit on a sofa together and breathe in time with each other, serene, warm and loving, enjoying a companionable silence. I was starting to look too much like my father, so I smudged a little Ocean Spray under my eyes and set off to research cultural resistance to Nazism in 1930s Germany.

Ocean Spray proved to be a tidal wave.

The librarian leaned forward over her desk and gazed directly into my Oceanic eyes. We resembled malicious cats taking up strange positions in an attempt to work out why the other might be an adversary. It was only eyeliner. We sort of stared each other out. She was doing something weird to signal her disapproval. It involved moving the muscles of her chin and lips so that her nose crinkled and her nostrils became bigger. I was glad she was not armed with a pistol.

I'd never discussed my research with my translator, who had more or less disappeared, as had Luna. I had not yet met her. Ursula told me that her daughter was sleeping in the flat of one of the radiologists at the hospital because she had signed up for extra training.

'Blood transfusion training,' she said curtly.

Ursula had not yet forgiven me for forgetting the tin of pineapple.

I was lonely but Rainer was good company. He took me to

bookshops and theatre shows and introduced me to some of his punk friends in the church group.

One night, when I was walking home from the library, I became aware that a man was following me. Tall and muscular, he walked on the opposite side of the road, always in step with my step. Obviously, my Oceanic eyes had been reported to the authorities. When I stopped to buy a version of a hot dog called Ketwurst, he waited for me by a lamp post. Every now and again he would light a cigarette, take two puffs and stub it out again. He wore a heavy grey coat, his mousy hair falling to his shoulders. When I limped, he limped. When I stopped to gaze at the destination on a tram, he stopped to gaze at a hole in the pavement. As I had learned from that very first walk with Walter on the day I arrived, he had infinite patience. His pale blue eyes were on me, that was for sure, but I did not regard his gaze as sinister. If anything he was ashamed and embarrassed at being told to stalk me. His heart wasn't in it. At one point I stamped my boot and said 'Magic' out loud, just to let him know that I did not blame him for being obliged to chase an insignificant fly like myself. I had deciphered the message in his eyes in the mirror and understood that he did not find me unsightly.

Walter turned up less covertly in the library at the end of the week, and requested we speak outside. Apparently, he now had a free weekend. Would I be available to travel with him to the family dacha on the outskirts of the city?

It was the season for mushrooms. If we were lucky we could 'harvest' some of them for dinner.

'I would like that very much, Walter.'

Out of the blue, he asked if I had a lover back home.

'Well, I did,' I replied, 'but she doesn't think I'm a serious contender.'

'Oh, why is that?'

'I don't know. She's mostly focused on her career.'

'What is her work?'

'She's an art student.'

'What kind of art?'

'Photography.'

'What kind of photographs?'

I was embarrassed because I did not know how to talk about Jennifer's art and I did not want to tell him that as far as I knew, most of her photographs were of myself. I did not understand those either, except for the one titled 'Saul at His Desk'. I still remembered Walter's reproachful tone when Rainer told him about his sister's girlfriend having her camera confiscated and the film being exposed by the authorities. It was quite an odd moment. I suppose his tone was fogged at the edges because he didn't really believe in the worth of the words he was saying. Jennifer believed in the worth of her photographs, though she did not believe in the worth of my words when they involved anything to do with her. I began to wonder what it took to believe in anything at all. God or Peace or a Classless Society? Perhaps it took magic.

'And how is the walking?' Walter gestured in a general sort of way to my feet. 'Are you still lame?'

I closed my eyes and touched the ends of my hair, which is what I always do when I am overwhelmed.

'Walter, if you're going to follow me around, you will know all about that.'

9

The weeds at the side of the road outside the dacha had been cut and bundled. Walter told me he planned to give them to the farmer to add to animal feed. It was raining hard as we walked around his allotment. He wanted to show me the vegetables he was cultivating, particularly the cabbages and potatoes. 'You can grow a lot of potatoes by planting potatoes.' Walter seemed pleased about the rain because he had recently put a new roof on the dacha. All the hammering had irritated one of the neighbours who used to be a broadcaster on state television, so he hoped the hard work had been worth it. His jeans and T-shirt were soaking wet, so was his hair, but he did not want to share my umbrella. I felt very English and uptight hanging on to it anyway, so I chucked it on the grass and stood closer to him as the rain pelted down. He wanted me to tell him about the graffiti on the west side of the Wall. Obviously he had never seen it – what did I think?

I couldn't tell him what I was thinking, because he had been following me home from the library. Instead, I told him how I grew three types of tomato in Britain.

'I've planted the usual plum, then San Marzano and the big ones, Costoluto Fiorentino.'

'What kind of soil?' Walter was curious. He did not see me as a tomato grower and neither did I.

'I grow the tomatoes in Suffolk, an East Anglian county in England.'

He did not believe me and neither did I totally believe myself. I had planted three types of tomato in another time. Someone had planted the tomatoes with me in the future soil of East Anglia. His hair is silver and he wears it in a bun on top of his head. His fingernails are bitten down. We are kneeling on the earth, his fingers on my back, massaging my spine while he tells me we should plant the apple trees before it rains and the fields flood.

The rain seemed to encourage Walter to talk. He told me he was thinking of starting a honeybee farm.

'How are you going to do that?'

He would begin with just one or two hives and put them where there was nectar, near the pollen of flowering plants. There would have to be shade and sun but no wind.

'My sister has misgivings. She is very prone to screaming when a bee lands on her arm. She is a nurse and always ready with her tweezers to take out the sting.'

'Perhaps you should keep a cat instead?'

'Agh.' He shook his head. 'Don't talk about cats. Luna has a phobia about cats.'

Every now and again he bent down to rip a dead leaf from a plant.

'So far, we have been talking about potatoes and cabbage, bees and cats and tomatoes,' he said. 'So now let's speak quietly in the rain about the ashes in your matchbox. You want to bury your father in my garden?'

'Yes.'

'Go ahead.'

I stood there in the rain, unable to move. I could not bring myself to bury my father. I suddenly felt light-headed and drowsy. I lifted my head to the sky and opened my mouth to the rain. As if it were an opiate, perhaps morphine, as if it could numb some sort of undisclosed suffering. Walter picked up the umbrella I had thrown on the grass.

I think he was trying to say he was sorry for me.

*

When the rainstorm was over, Walter took me mushrooming in the woods. For some reason he was wearing a trilby hat made from felt. It didn't look that good but he seemed very attached to it. Walter knew where the mushrooms would be bursting through the soil.

'They have deep root systems under the ground and they like the rain, so when we see one poke its head above ground we must first identify if it is poisonous.'

He told me he was wearing the hat so he could duck under the branches of trees that created shade for the fungi. He wanted to teach me everything about mushrooms. While he spoke, he sometimes touched my arm for emphasis as we walked deeper into the woods.

'When people camp here they sometimes get ill and even die because they have eaten the deadly ones.' There was apparently an interesting man who ran the local pharmacy. He could identify all the mushrooms and he offered a professional mushroom-identification service. I had rolled up my shirtsleeves but Walter told me to cover my arms because the ticks were bloodthirsty. The smaller mushrooms were tastier than the bigger ones, so that's what we were looking for. If there were frosts it would be the end of the season, but we were apparently in luck because it was still warm.

We were both now squatting over a cluster of mushrooms.

'This one is likely to be poisonous.' He turned it over with a twig, both of us concealed under the heavy branches of a tall dripping tree. Walter leaned forward to look at it more closely, which meant our heads were touching. Rain dripped down our cheeks. And then he kissed me on my lips. When I did not move away, both of us still squatting over the poisonous mushroom, he bit my lower lip, gently, then fiercely. His second kiss was less polite, his fingers tracing my cheekbones and eyebrows. The damp earth and the cries of small animals and the musky smell of the mushrooms and the taste of him were the sort of life I wanted. I was electrified by Walter Müller. When we pulled apart he said in German, 'This one is such a beauty,' but I didn't know if he was referring to the mushroom or myself.

As the light faded that night, we closed the curtains in the dacha. Our clothes were still damp; we had been drinking schnapps and had nearly finished the bottle. Both of us were drunk.

'When I first saw you, Saul, at the station in Friedrichstraße, you were like an angel, full lips, high cheekbones, blue eyes, a classical body like a statue, but then I discovered your wings were wounded. I had to carry your bag and you became human.'

It was raining again. We could hear water running off the roof.

'I was trying hard to be a man you could respect,' I replied.

'And when we got home you said anything that came into your head.'

He was speaking in German and I was too drunk to understand all of what he was saying, but then he changed the subject, no warning, his authoritarian voice coming back like a spectre lurking inside him. He asked if I wanted him to help translate the lecture I was to deliver on Monday to eight students on a cultural exchange programme. No, I told him, it was straightforward. He looked at me in a certain way and I agreed without speaking to something I had understood when we exchanged looks in the mirror of his mother's apartment. I said yes with my eyes and I reached out (again) to pull him closer. Perhaps I was becoming the cat and less of the mouse. I felt his physical strength when we were lying on the floor. His desire was like a lamp, an old-fashioned lamp with a wick and paraffin, smouldering, flickering, his body bigger than mine, his thighs harder, his skin pale, so very pale. I was tanned compared to Walter Müller.

When he took off his jeans, he actually stood up to fold them and place them on a chair. He did not walk towards me again, he just stood there by the chair, which forced me to walk towards him. I was terrified because it was proof that I wanted him. I wanted this as much as he wanted it, but he kept giving me the opportunity to walk away.

I don't know why he did that. He was taunting me, but the taunt was something like, yes, you are choosing this, you want it too.

Later, when we were lying on the floor on our backs, his arm across my chest, I realized the temperature had dropped. It had suddenly become very cold. He asked about the bruise on my thigh which was the size of a saucer. When I explained it was from the near collision on Abbey Road, he kissed the bruise and then he kissed my lips, which were not bruised. I could hear my own frantic heartbeat pounding in my ears.

'Walter, I have to ask you something.'

'Go ahead.'

The rain was now falling hard. The sound of water everywhere.

'If we had been friends earlier, say 1941, I would have had to ask you to hide me.'

'Yes.'

'Would you have helped me?'

'Of course. No doubt about it.'

'And what if we had been at school together and you discovered I was forbidden from swimming with you at the public pools. Would you still have been my friend?'

'More than that, Saul. I would have done everything I could to save you.'

The questions I was asking Walter were not fair. I understood they were taboo questions, but what was I supposed to do with these questions?

I would have done everything I could to save you.

I believed Walter Müller's words. They expressed themselves to me in sound. Like a typewriter hammering in my head.

Would you still have been my friend?

More than that, Saul. I would have done everything I could to save you.

At the same time, I knew he was following me when I visited the British embassy to have a cup of British tea and read the newspapers. I had seen him smoking outside the building every time I was there. I knew his heart was not in it, but he had to save himself.

*

60

Walter seemed to have no shame about his naked body. He walked around the kitchen making coffee. There was no milk, no sugar, but he had bought some meat which he planned to cook with sour apples and potatoes as soon as he had sobered up. It was cold, despite Ursula's news of the young people of Leipzig cooling off in the fountain. Walter was only a few years older than myself, but he seemed very much older. Protective of his mother and sister. More domesticated. Kinder. Good at gardening, cooking and putting up a roof. I wrapped a blanket over my shoulders. While he looked for sugar he asked again about my late father, avoiding the subject of the matchbox with its teaspoon of forlorn ash.

'My father raised my brother and me in the spirit of socialism and peace. We were to be highly principled and never exploit anyone to make ourselves richer. He was an internationalist, not a nationalist, he declared his solidarity with working people around the world. All the same I think he wanted to purge me from the family.'

I was now shivering under the blanket.

'As far as he was concerned, I was always on trial.'

In reply, Walter pointed to my pearl necklace.

'I expect it belonged to your mother?'

'Yes.'

I told him how when she died I had asked my father for her necklace. Pearls absorb the heat of the body and become part of it. I had never given much thought to a pearl belonging to a gender. If I had to fight in a war I'd have to take off my pearls, so obviously I was for world peace all round.

Walter told me that his parents were divorced and his father was a trade union steward. They got on all right, but he was closer to Ursula, who was 'happier in her mind'. He told me to be discreet about our weekend in the dacha. He was considered by his university to be politically reliable and he had high qualifications. All the same he could be removed from his job if it was thought that his sexuality in any way threatened to destabilize the regime.

'I understand.'

'As for burying your father's ashes in my garden, you will have to consult with my sister. This is her dacha as much as mine.'

'I would like to see you again, Walter.'

'Yes?'

'Yes.'

All those yeses were the same as him starting and stopping when we were murmuring and gasping on the floor.

Yes?

Yes.

Yes?

Maybe the Stasi were right to wave their pencils over the lyrics of pop songs.

Yeah yeah yeah. What could that possibly mean?

I was still shivering under the blanket.

'You English do not like being naked.' Walter was now peeling three tiny, gnarled potatoes with intense focus. 'But I am going to take you swimming in one of our best lakes and you will be naked for this swimming because it is unhygienic to wear clothes in water.'

I asked him to tell me about Luna. Where was she and why had I not yet met her?

'Oh, you will meet Luna!' He started to laugh, as he always did when he spoke about his sister. Apparently, she refused to stay in the dacha alone. She was an insomniac, a nocturnal person. And she had many fears. Mostly about animals. The first, but not strongest, fear was the wolves that had migrated from western Poland and sometimes roamed the countryside looking for sheep. There were good reasons, he said, why wolves howl at the moon. Raising their heads helps carry sound further. Their howl is a form of long-distance communication and it conveys all kinds of information. Luna was not scared that a wolf would maul her, she was terrified of the way it raised its head.

*

The meat he had bought for our dinner turned out to be liver. I watched him rinse the tubes and tendons under the tap. Are there tendons in liver?

'I like to cook. So does Katrin.'

'Who is Katrin?'

'Luna. I will leave the mushrooms for her.'

When I stood up with the cup of coffee in my hand and started to pace the kitchen, trying to keep warm, I managed to trip over a pile of old boots on the floor. The cup fell from my hand and the coffee spilled on to the jeans that had been folded and placed on the chair. Walter threw down the liver and ran to the chair, grabbed his jeans and swiftly carried them to the sink. He wet a cloth and started to rub at the black stain on the denim. He was shouting, 'Fuck fuck fuck.' I realized the jeans were Wrangler's, hard to get in the GDR, and that he must have worn them specially for me.

I was mortified. I didn't know what to do.

'You can have my jeans, Walter. You are bigger than I am but they will fit you.'

Later, much later, when the sun was coming up and we were lying in bed, he said, 'Okay, thank you for the jeans. Accepted.'

In a small way I felt I had made up for forgetting to bring the tin of pineapple. He suggested I should spend next weekend with Luna here at the dacha because she was scared to be alone. His sister had promised to look after the elderly neighbour who was unwell, but she was frightened of the jaguar.

'I thought she was scared of the wolves?'

'Yes. And the jaguar.'

'You mean a jaguar like a leopard?'

'Yes.' He was lying on his side, smoking a cigarette and laughing again.

Apparently, a black jaguar had been spotted near the dacha some years back. No one knew where it had come from. There had been

63

photographs in all the newspapers. It was a mystery because jaguars are usually from South America or Arizona. It liked to climb trees and pounce on its prey, so now Luna would not walk under trees. Walter was still laughing.

'But most of all,' he said, 'jaguars like water.'

Apparently, this East German jaguar had also been spotted hunting for fish in a lake. There was an idea it was a female jaguar and that it was pregnant. So someone else wrote to the newspapers to say baby jaguars had been spotted in a forest near the lake.

While Walter spoke at length about jaguars, I was looking at a calendar pinned on to the wooden walls of the dacha, celebrating the tenth anniversary of the first joint Soviet–East German space flight.

'You know, Walter, I think I have seen that jaguar.'

'So, you're crazy like Luna? Where did you see it?'

'It's silver,' I said. 'It's not black.'

'You saw the jaguar here or near the university?'

'I don't know.'

He stubbed out his cigarette in an old sardine tin.

'When you meet my sister, it's best to tell her we're just friends. Okay with you?'

'Okay with me.'

He pointed to a pair of pale pink ballet shoes lying under the table.

'They belong to Luna. Sometimes when she can't sleep she dances in the night to calm herself.'

After we cleaned the dacha and locked the front door, I saw a white Wartburg parked opposite Walter's allotment. Two men were sitting inside it, smoking and talking. Walter did not seem to notice the men in the car when I whispered they were there. He and I had a weird moment on the doorstep. I said, 'Stop typing, Walter,' and he replied, 'You really are crazy, Saul,' but as he put the keys in his pocket, I saw his eyes flick in the direction of the Wartburg that was apparently not there.

10

When I at last met Luna, she was upside down.

She was brushing her long hair in endless repetitions near the ceramic stove in the apartment and reading a book at the same time. I couldn't see her face because she had bent her head towards the floor so her light blond hair touched the carpet. She was reading 'Howl' by the poet Allen Ginsberg. I asked her how she'd got hold of her copy.

'Rainer, of course.'

I thought she had a lisp at first but later she told me she'd had a tiny sliver of chocolate under her tongue and talking too much would have spoilt her pleasure. Her aunt from the West had sent her a birthday package and she was trying to make the chocolate last. She was in her mid twenties and petite, quite different from her muscular older brother. When she flicked her head up again, her light blond hair, the colour of a cloud, was electric from all the brushing. It fell down to her narrow waist. When she finally looked at me, I had the impression she had been taking her time, as if preparing herself to gaze at something painful, or thrilling, or frightening. Her eyes were pale green, her skin luminous. Walter's features were not as defined as Luna's. It was as if his face was still becoming his face, he was not quite himself, which was very attractive to me. And so was the way he looked at me all the time. He couldn't take his eyes off me, which I confess I found flattering. It was the other way around with Luna, who couldn't bear to look at me. She shook my hand in a formal manner and asked if I had enjoyed the weekend in the dacha with her brother.

'Yes, thank you. We collected mushrooms and drank something strong. It was a restful break from my research.'

'You're wearing his jeans,' she said. 'They're too big for you.'

'Yes. I gave him my Wrangler's.'

Luna's green eyes were like mirrors. I could see myself smiling in both her eyes, as if I had become a double self, which in a sense was right. I was learning to not be myself in the GDR.

'Why did you do this exchange? Wrangler for Wrangler?'

'I spilled my coffee over his jeans.'

She laughed and flung up her arms in a sort of ballet position. Her raised arms made an O shape in the air.

At the same time, she sucked the sliver of chocolate as it melted under her tongue.

'You should have given them to me. I am thinner than he is and so are you. His jeans are falling off your hips. Did you only bring one pair of jeans with you?'

I had brought an unlikely suit and two ties with me to East Berlin, as well as two pairs of jeans. I had worn the suit and tie to the library and to give my lecture to the students on the cultural exchange programme. At home in London, I obviously owned many pairs of jeans, but I was enjoying becoming less of the man from the West, which my jeans broadcast to everyone here. Yet Luna's question about the things I might have brought with me from the well-stocked shops of London made me uneasy.

It was as if she was waiting for me to give her something. And actually, I was about to.

'Hang on, Luna. I've got a gift for you.'

I rummaged around in my grey canvas sling bag and took out the envelope Jennifer had sent me with the Abbey Road photographs inside it. There were three of them and I paused as I chose the one I wanted Luna to have.

In the end I passed her the photograph of myself in mid-stride crossing the road barefoot, my hands in the pockets of the white Navy suit from Laurence Corner.

'Sorry it's not the real Beatles,' I said.

She held it carefully in both hands and stared at it for a long time.

'I must get to Liverpool,' she eventually whispered to the photograph. The ends of her electric hair fell over the black-and-white stripes of the zebra crossing.

'I know I will find work in a hospital. I will earn money to buy my fish dinner in Penny Lane like in the song.'

She lifted the photograph to her lips and kissed it.

'Thank you, Saul.' She pointed to my white suit from Laurence Corner.

'What is that?'

I stood behind her, peering over her shoulder at the photograph.

She was pointing to three small stains on the pockets of the jacket.

'I think it's blood.'

'That's what I thought too,' she said.

I told her about nearly getting run over on the day I posed for that photograph, how I fell on to the zebra using my hands to protect myself and how my cut knuckle wouldn't stop bleeding.

'Who made the photo? It's great. Yes, it's a really good photo.'

'My girlfriend took it.'

'What's her name?'

'Actually, she's my ex-girlfriend.'

'But she still has a name.' Luna's teeth were crooked and snarled together, except for the gap between the front two.

'Jennifer.'

'So what went wrong?'

'I don't know. To be honest I don't understand what went wrong.'

'Did she not notice your jacket was stained with blood?'

I shrugged. For some reason I did not want to tell her how Jennifer and I had gone back to her flat and made love and that she hadn't

67

commented on my white suit because we were more interested in taking off our clothes.

'Are you sad to lose her?' Luna walked to the other end of the room, the photograph still in her hand.

It was a question I had not directly asked myself. Not even in English. Now I was required to answer it in German. Was I sad to lose Jennifer? How did I know if I was sad?

In a way it was a relief. And yet I had asked her to marry me, to leave her friends and pack up her stuff, to change her address and redirect her post and come and live her life with me. I had asked her to consider that plan and three seconds later she had dumped me. So then, I reasoned, if I had wanted her to leave her life with her friends and also the beloved sauna that was the exotic free gift that came with the flat in Hamilton Terrace, to bring her clothes and shoes, her kettle and pots and her cameras and all the apparatus of her work, I must be sad that we had separated.

Why had she insisted it was over between us? It was as if Jennifer had punished me for an unconscious crime she knew I wanted to commit and had ended our relationship because it was going to end anyway. She had already dumped me once, before my offer of marriage. On that occasion her fingers were covered in oil paint. We had agreed to meet in Foyles bookshop on the Charing Cross Road, which was next door to her art school. As I lifted my arms to embrace her, she had lunged at my chest and thumped her hands on my white T-shirt so that it was stained with orange paint. 'Not orange,' she said, 'it's called Permanent Yellow Deep.' I had only known her for three months at that time. The queasy thing about Jennifer Moreau was that she was only in her early twenties but she possessed a sense of purpose that I myself did not possess. It gave her confidence even when she did not know what she was doing. She had told me with tremendous certainty that she was going to wash her paintbrushes for the last time and take up a camera instead. What had I done that was really so bad? Was I supposed to mourn the loss of her paintbrushes?

The night before I had danced at a club with one of her friends. Nothing had happened between us, except that I had placed my hands on Claudia's hips. 'No,' Jennifer had said, 'your hands were under her shirt on her hips.' I wondered if I was not supposed to notice that Claudia had a body when we danced together. I did notice that plenty of male art students were interested in Jennifer, but how could they not be enchanted by her beauty? When I told her she looked like Lee Miller, the American photographer, Jennifer replied, 'That doesn't mean anything.'

Luna was still waiting for my reply. She was peering at the photograph, holding it close to her face and then moving it further away.

'Yes,' I said. 'I am sad.'

I intuited that Luna would have a better opinion of me if I was sad. I touched the ends of my hair and closed my eyes.

'Are you okay, Saul?'

'Yes.'

Was I okay?

What would the truthful reply to that question be? Yes and No. The Yes and the No existing in parallel, like the black-and-white stripes of the zebra crossing on Abbey Road. But what if the No was bigger than the Yes? A lot bigger. And then I crossed the road?

I opened my eyes.

I had not yet told Luna about forgetting to bring the tin of pineapple and I was dreading the moment I would have to confess. And I was missing Walter. For the first time I wondered if he had a lover. Why wouldn't he have a lover? Ursula had told me that Walter would be coming to the apartment that evening. He had promised to fix a leak in the neighbour's flat above hers and had complained that he would have to move a heavy table to position it under the leak. The ladder was broken so he would have to stand on the table to reach the ceiling. I missed Walter. I missed Jennifer. I was also missing writing the paper I had begun in London on the psychology of male tyrants, starting with the way Stalin flirted by throwing balls of bread at the woman he desired. I knew I must not even think about this paper here, that would be a thought crime, though I reckoned I could talk to Rainer about it. I was desperate not to be left alone with Luna, mostly because of the tin of pineapple. Where was Ursula? She was later than usual coming home from work.

Luna was still interested in how many pairs of jeans I had brought with me to East Berlin. She was so persistent I eventually grabbed the one pair of Levi's I had brought with me and carried them from my bedroom like a trophy back to her.

'Oh, thank you, Saul!' She was pleased and excited.

I would have to spend the rest of my time in the GDR dressed in the unlikely suit or Walter's stained Wrangler's.

'I'll try them on,' she said, unzipping her skirt. As she stood in front of me in her pants and stepped into the jeans, I turned my back on her and sat at the small table next to the lamp. I opened my book and started to make notes in the margin.

'Do you have a belt, Saul?'

I told her I had only brought one belt with me.

'Do you have another pair in a smaller size?'

I told her I did not.

When her mother returned from work they started whispering to each other. Someone else must have come in with her because I could hear pots being banged about in the kitchen. Ursula was being asked to give an opinion on the jeans. After a while I noticed a blue dress hanging on a hook on the wall, and also, draped on the hook, a stethoscope. Ursula pointed to the tiny wooden train that Walter had been trying to mend. It was perched on top of her bag.

'It's well made, no?'

I was bored and irritated as I tried to read at the table.

'You are working now, Saul?'

I nodded and turned back to my book.

'What are you writing on the pages?'

70

'I'm making notes on the economic and social conditions that led to the second Russian revolution of October 1917.'

'Feel free to smoke. We have three ashtrays in this apartment. By the way, I think the October revolution took place in November.'

She grabbed Luna's hand and both of them disappeared into the bathroom. I could hear them discussing the Levi's and how best to alter them to fit tiny Luna so she could wear them in every month of the year.

Every now and again I glanced at the pin-up calendar, the colour photograph of the woman in a gold bikini. Her presence was a strange interruption in this room, what with her gold fingernails and false eyelashes, her impersonation of a smile and fake erotic allure. She looked tired and strained. I couldn't understand the appeal of this calendar to the two women who lived here, a mother and daughter. It occurred to me that if there was a listening device in this room, it would be hidden under that calendar and not the mirror, as I had first thought. I could still hear pots being banged about in the kitchen. At the same time, Ursula and Luna were talking loudly in the bathroom.

A man was standing in the kitchen. He seemed to be reaching for something on the top shelf. His T-shirt had parted from the belt of his jeans. I saw his naked back and I knew he was Walter. At that moment Luna and Ursula walked back into the living room. Luna started to parade up and down the carpet in my jeans, which had been taken in at the waist with safety pins. I shivered. The same sort of shiver as when a cold stethoscope is placed on warm skin. I heard the sound of matches being struck in the kitchen and the man, who was definitely Walter, mutter, 'Oh shit.' Ursula's dyed red hair had been curled and she was wearing a flared polka-dot skirt. When she saw me looking at her, she smiled.

'You have only seen me in my work clothes.'

'True.'

'You have not asked me where I work.'

'Where do you work, Ursula?'

'In a factory. I make fish hooks. It's Luna's birthday today. She's twenty-six.'

Ursula put two fingers in her mouth and let out a loud whistle. Walter walked out of the kitchen, holding a birthday cake in his hands. It was crowded with pale pink candles, a multitude of tiny flames. He started to sing 'Happy Birthday' and Ursula joined in.

They had worked out a harmony for the very last 'happy birthday to you', after which Luna blew out the candles and began to tear them from the cake. She was acting like someone much younger than her new twenty-six years, dropping each candle on the floor as she reached for another one. Her mother and brother laughed indulgently. Now that the cake was shorn of its candles, she peered at it from all angles. The cake was circled with peaches. Tinned peaches. She took the knife from Walter's hand and with feral energy cut into it, dropping the knife on the floor as she scooped up a wedge of cake and stuffed it into her mouth. Her face was smeared with cream and slivers of peach and then she opened her mouth and spat out the cake. Maybe she even howled.

I heard her shout the word *ananas*, which is German for pineapple. She burst into tears.

'Peaches taste like soap.'

Luna did not so much run out of the room as balletically run out of the room, still crying, and then she banged the door. Walter was left stranded with the peach cake in his hands. Ursula bent down to pick the candles off the floor. I did not know what to do with myself. There was nowhere to escape because my bedroom was right next to Luna's room. Walter was looking at me. Deep into my eyes. He was always looking at me and I think he could see everything that was good and bad and sad in me. Jennifer was always looking at me too, but I don't know what she saw because there was always the lens of

72

her camera between us. Walter was laughing, as usual. When Ursula stood up she was laughing too.

'That's our Luna.' She gazed at me slightly flirtatiously while she lit a cigarette.

'Luna is short for Lunatic.'

This time I laughed.

'Do you want a beer, Saul?' Walter put the evil cake down on the table and rested his arm across his mother's shoulders.

'Yes,' Ursula said, 'I think we all need a beer.'

We could hear Luna crying in her bedroom.

Later that night, after Walter had left, I saw Luna standing mournfully in the bathroom, looking at herself in the mirror above the basin.

'I'm sorry. Did I ruin your birthday, Luna?'

'Yes and no.' She turned on the tap and nudged the door shut with her foot. Two seconds later she opened it again.

'I'm not crying about pineapple. I'm crying because Rainer has been given a passport that allows him to travel to the West four days a year. I want to see Penny Lane in Liverpool. And I am stuck here.'

She picked up a bar of soap and threw it at me and slammed the door again.

Then she opened the door.

'Give me back the soap.'

Her waist was tiny but her voice was huge.

I spent all night thinking about Walter. When I left East Berlin and made my way to West Berlin, we would be divided by a wall. Yet, if Luna was to be believed, Rainer could walk through that wall four times a year. I was missing Walter. It was a physical longing to be close to his body. I did not want to sleep in this small chaste bed, I wanted to sleep by his side. I felt I knew him better with his eyes closed. His thoughts could move freely between the sky and the horizon, he could roam the earth with no restrictions, our legs entwined in the darkness of the night.

I lay in my cold single bed and wrote Walter a letter in which I declared my deepest feelings for him. In high emotion I searched for words, lying on the hip that was not bruised, propped up on my elbow. I described how I wanted to touch him and how I had always wanted to see the Baltic Sea in winter. My letter was an invitation for him to accompany me on that journey. At the same time, I heard my father's voice speak to me in the GDR. His Master's Voice was loud and harsh. That night, I knocked him to the ground and sat astride his chest, my hands around his throat. I keep pressing until he stopped breathing and his regime was over.

11

Not all lakes are equal. Walter explained this concept to me as we walked through the forest towards the shore of the lake that was reserved for VIPs.

'We have permission to swim here because you are our bridge between East and West and will write a report about our economic miracle.'

We walked in step, side by side through a cloud of mosquitoes. Walter had been given a yellow slip of paper to hand to the guard who had been standing outside a security hut halfway between the train station and the forest. I was not paying attention because of what had happened when we were waiting for the train. Walter had said something to me of great importance. It was not exactly a whisper. He had spoken quietly near my ear. A whisper suggests a secret is being transmitted and encourages the curiosity of others. He had told me that he loved me. He said it very simply. As if he were carrying a bag of brown coal up from the cellar.

Now he was being a tour guide. Apparently, Erich Honecker swam in this lake, under the protection of his personal guards. The summer villas in the surrounding area belonged to the party's most important officials. As we walked through the forest I glimpsed a small island of trees in the middle of the lake. Walter confessed it was sometimes hard to speak in English, so he hoped he made sense when he spoke to me. I assumed he wanted me to know that he had meant the words he had quietly spoken in English on the platform of the train station.

'I have to speak English in a way that does not give it my personality,' he replied. 'All translation is like that. The personality of the translator has to hide.'

'Are you saying you hide inside all the languages you translate? Like hiding in a forest?'

He shrugged. 'It's not so simple.' And then he laughed.

'You are a lightweight, Saul. I received your letter. Thank you.'

He flicked a cigarette out of its pack. I lit it for him with my Zippo. My fingers fleetingly touched his hands, which were cupped around the cigarette.

Walter looked smarter than usual. His hair was washed and he had shaved.

I wondered if he had made the effort for me, because that morning I had also shaved with extra care. My hair had grown longer while I was in the East. It now reached beyond my shoulders. Luna had given me an elastic band to make a ponytail. 'You look like a girl with your hair down.' She was biting her lip as she watched me experiment with a ponytail, but after a while I gave up. Actually, it hurt to touch my head. I had a headache most days. When I had washed my hair that morning, a memory of my mother suddenly flashed into my head. She had been given two bottles of a shampoo called Prell. It was thick and green, like washing-up liquid. There was an advertisement for this shampoo that she had learned off by heart.

'Touch your hair. Close your eyes. What does it make you think?' The idea was that if you touched your hair after washing it with Prell, it would make you think of silk. Any time my brother and I were upset, she would say, 'Touch your hair. Close your eyes. What does it make you think?' In the GDR it was not necessarily wise to say what you thought. Yet I believed that Walter had said what he thought on the platform of that train station and that it was my letter

76

declaring my deepest feelings that had prompted him to speak of his own feelings.

I asked him if he had a lover.

'In a way I do.'

I began to understand more about the way Walter spoke in English and German. He did not speak spontaneously, certainly not the first thoughts that came to mind. Perhaps he said the third thought that came to mind. It was not a matter of finding a flow but finding a way to stop the flow. I asked him again if he had a lover.

'Yes. I have a companion.'

I punched his arm and he punched my arm. We understood the punch but it was not how our bodies wanted to speak to each other. A punch? No. When we were alone in the dacha he spoke freely with his body. And that is something I have never done. I have never had a free conversation with my body. I have silenced my lovers with my body and controlled the kind of conversation they wished to have with their own body. I have never been free. I have pretended to be more tender or turned on than I felt, or more aggressive than I felt, and when we came close to something more intimate, I pulled away, interrupted the physical conversation. Yet with Walter, I was free with my body. This was to do with the way we had talked on the first day he met me at the station. It was true that my wings were wounded. It was true that I had no idea how to endure being alive and everything that comes with it. Responsibility. Love. Death. Sex. Loneliness. History. I knew he did not hold my tears against me. That was a big thing to know.

It was a warm day. The scent from the pine trees and the blue sky and Walter at my side seemed to heighten my lust and misery and happiness. The odd thing was that those words, lust, misery, happiness, were the words in a title of one of Jennifer's portraits of me. I wondered if I was starting to become the man she had seen from behind her lens.

I said very softly to Walter, 'I will miss you when I leave.' He did

77

not reply for a while, but then he shrugged. 'I am happy to offer you my comradeship.' He raised his left eyebrow and looked up at the tree. A small wooden platform had been built in its branches. A uniformed guard was standing on the planks, smoking a cigarette. Was Walter being cautious or was he unwriting his first thought? He had not censored his first thought when he'd touched me. His hands had been fluent in every language, his lips soft, his body hard.

We were now walking along a pathway that wound around the lake.

'What about Jennifer? Do you miss her?'

It was startling to hear Jennifer's name spoken out loud in that forest, so far away from my old life, even though I was thinking about her. Luna must have talked to her brother about the photograph of Abbey Road.

'Jennifer is clever and ambitious.' The way I said those words sounded like a reproach and I was slightly ashamed.

I couldn't tell Walter that as well as starting to feel the words with which she had titled one of her portraits of her main subject – me – there were new images in my mind that resembled Jennifer's photographs, images from another geography, another time. I was convinced that Jennifer had not yet taken those photographs, which I saw like slides in a carousel. A cherry tree in Massachusetts, America. Someone standing under the tree. That person might be myself. Jennifer was there, too. Her hair had turned white. Someone else was there, but the image was blurred.

'I sometimes miss Jennifer.'

We took off our clothes and left them on the shore of the clear green lake. I felt something touch me, like a butterfly near my neck. Walter had slipped his finger under my pearls. I told him I never took off my necklace, not even to swim. As I waded into the water I felt sand between my toes. I kept on walking. The sand was still there and I was now up to my neck in the water.

'Lift your feet, Saul.'

'I am avoiding the turtle,' I replied.

'There are no turtles in this lake.'

I think the turtle came from another lake in another time, but I was still reluctant to lift my feet from the comforting sand. Walter dunked his head in the water and I eventually lifted my feet. We swam past the tall trees towards the island. After about twenty minutes, I was shivering. The water was surprisingly cold. Walter was waving to someone. There was no one there. Yet he had seen someone who was there. The calm, still water broke into a gentle froth.

Walter shouted across the lake in German: 'Good morning, Wolf.'

We swam together towards the invisible man called Wolf.

The man was on his back, kicking his legs, whirling his arms. He opened his eyes. Dark brown eyes. Slanted at the corners. He was not looking at me but I was looking at him because I had seen him before. I was treading water now, out of my depth, but I was sure he was the man who had nearly run me over on Abbey Road in London. Walter tapped me on the shoulder.

'Wolf is the director of our university.'

Wolf fleetingly opened his brown slanting eyes again. He was looking at Walter, not at me. There was something in that look that made me think he was Walter's lover. As if to prove it, Walter swam behind the floating man's head, gripped both his wrists and stretched Wolf's arms behind his head, as if to improve his swimming stroke.

'It's true,' Wolf said in German, 'I am stiffer than I used to be.' He turned his gaze towards me.

'We Germans invented all the big movements of the twentieth century. Phenomenology from Heidegger and Hegel, communism from Marx and Engels. So you will have to excuse us for being a little stiff in our limbs – we have been busy.'

His dark slanting eyes closed again, but not before his gaze had momentarily wandered to the necklace of white pearls I never took off, not to make love or to write essays or to teach my students or to cross the road.

Yet how could Wolf be the same person who nearly ran me over? The man on Abbey Road was English. *How old are you, Soorl? Can you tell me where you live?*

A fish flicked against my ankles.

'I wonder,' I asked in German, 'if we have met before in London?'

Wolf's slanting eyes peeped open. Walter stood behind him, cradling his head in the water.

'No. I have never been to London.'

He started to kick his legs and Walter let go of his head.

Later, when we were making our way through the forest towards the station, Walter pointed to a car, a Trabant parked under the pine trees.

'The director has offered to give us a lift home.'

'I would rather catch the train.'

'What's up, Saul?'

'I've had some bad experiences with cars and I can't see how it would get better in a Trabi.'

The guard standing on his wooden platform in the tree was now looking at us both. His expression was not aggressive or vigilant. He looked as if he was daydreaming amongst the pines and spruces. Walter poked my ribs. Wolf was making his way towards us, his towel rolled under his arm.

I had no choice but to travel home with Wolf and Walter. I sat on the back seat and pretended to sleep, but I was aware that Walter had draped his arm over Wolf's shoulder. Wolf raised his head to glance at me in the rear-view mirror. He was driving with just one hand on the wheel. I kept my eyes on Walter's arm as if it were a traitor.

Walter's lips moved nearer Wolf's pink ear. He was speaking in German. Not a whisper but a low monotone.

'He has no political affiliations. He doesn't even vote.'

Wolf's laugh was more of a snort. His voice was a low monotone too.

'Your angel sleeping in the back seat writes you careless letters.'

'Yes,' Walter replied. 'He doesn't care about his own life so he doesn't care about the lives of others.'

It was true that Walter's eyes were on me all the time, but I trusted him because his hands were all over me too.

12

I could feel that something was wrong with Jennifer and that she wanted to get in touch with me. I tried three times to call her in Britain. The first couple of times I rang her flat in Hamilton Terrace at six in the evening British time. Claudia picked up the phone. When she heard my voice, she slammed the phone down. The second time she asked me what I wanted.

'I want Jennifer.'

'Well, she doesn't want you.' The phone went dead.

I knew that if Jennifer didn't want me, Claudia did, but she had to be loyal to Jennifer, who didn't much like Claudia anyway. She resented the way Claudia signalled her desire for her boyfriend. I could live without Claudia's desire for me, but life is more exciting to live with desire in it.

The next time I called at dawn, GDR time. The phone rang for a long time. Jennifer and her flatmates were probably asleep. The sauna would be switched off. The cat would be asleep too. There would be a bowl of seaweed soaking in water in the kitchen. Probably a pot of vegetable curry on the hob from the night before. Empty wine bottles. Chocolate wrappers. Maybe even the flapjacks that Claudia liked to bake, mixing the oats with honey, or sometimes with a thick golden syrup, often with raisins but never with walnuts because she discovered that I don't like them. Eventually, Saanvi answered.

She sounded pleased to hear from me, even though Jennifer apparently was not in.

'Where is she?'

'Don't know. She hasn't given me her schedule.'

'It's seven o'clock in the morning your time, Saanvi?'

'Yes.'

'So who else is in the flat with you?'

'Hey, Saul, have you picked up some tips from the Stasi?'

I could hear a door creak open in Hamilton Terrace. I was familiar with that door and its broken latch, the door of Jennifer's bedroom that opened on to the kitchen. It was always blowing open. I was certain that Jennifer had just woken up and was now standing next to Saanvi, so I changed the subject.

'How's it going with infinity?'

'Good, thanks.'

'Are you still writing your thesis on Georg Cantor?'

'Yep. He had a persecution complex.'

Someone was filling a kettle with water. I could hear the rustle of paper and Saanvi yawning.

'Listen to this, Saul. The French mathematician Henri Poincaré described Georg Cantor's work as "a malady, a perverse illness from which someday mathematics will be cured".'

It sounded like she was reading from a page of her dissertation.

'He died in a mental clinic in Germany.'

'Whereabouts in Germany, Saanvi?'

'Halle. Between Berlin and Göttingen. Handel was born in Halle too. So was the poet Heine. Are you anywhere near there?'

'No.'

'It used to produce salt in the tenth century. Cantor was working on a continuum problem just before his breakdown.'

'Saanvi, how is Jennifer?'

'She's brilliant.'

I heard a loud click and then two quieter clicks on the phone line as she spoke. It occurred to me that my call to Britain was being monitored. It was likely that someone was listening to this conversation about Georg Cantor and infinity.

'Saanvi, are you still there?'

'Yep.'

'Please tell Jennifer to come to the GDR to see its achievements for herself. Full employment, affordable housing, equal pay for women, free education and universal health care. These are great accomplishments and should never be erased from historic memory.'

The phone went dead. Saanvi was probably making herself and Jennifer a cup of tea while dividing zero into thirds.

The sound of a typewriter was going crazy in my head. I heard the keys hammering on to a sheet of thin paper placed in its carriage. It infuriated me, so I added a thought crime to my thoughts for the typewriter to record. Okay, I said to the typewriter, let me help you file your report. The GDR will lose legitimacy with its people due to extreme measures of coercion by authoritarian old men. Men like my father who built a wall between us. The wall was his masculinity. I jumped the wall and landed safely with a thump on the other side, having avoided his dogs, his mines, his guards, his barbed wire and everything else he put in my way to keep me under his thumb.

My father was sitting on a chair near the telephone.

'You're dead,' I whispered.

He laughed. 'Not yet.'

I could smell tinned mackerel on his breath.

13

I agreed to accompany Luna to the dacha for the weekend.

I did not want to be alone with her for a whole day and night, but after forgetting to buy the tin of pineapple, I felt I couldn't refuse. It seemed that although Luna had many phobias, including peaches and jaguars, she was at ease with blood, because in her job she worked with blood every day. That was why she had noticed the bloodstains on my white jacket in the Abbey Road photograph. While I made tea for myself and coffee for her, she gave me a lecture about blood. Apparently, the way blood works is that like a reliable train it transports all the nutrients and oxygen to our cells and then it also transports all the waste products away from our cells.

I glanced at the small bag of mushrooms that Walter and I had collected together. There were not that many of them because kissing had become a more enjoyable sport than harvesting fungi. He had hung the bag on a hook on the wall.

'It is certain, Saul,' Luna said, 'that you will have around five litres of blood in your body and the white blood cells will be fighting off infections. If you donate just half a litre of blood it can save up to three lives.'

She had plaited her long hair and pinned it up so that it lay in a serpentine coil on top of her head, and she was very taken with her new black pointed ankle boots in the style of the Beatles', two sizes too big for her small feet. They were Rainer's birthday gift to her. It was endearing to be given a lecture on blood by a nurse wearing imitation Beatle boots, her hair arranged in the style of a prima ballerina. She had taken ballet lessons from the age of four from a Russian dancer who was old now but used to run a ballet school in Moscow. Luna did not like tea. I had brought teabags with me to East Berlin, but there was a reproach in the way she took a sip from my cup to taste 'the English tea'.

'It smells like horse urine. But you drink tea all the time so I suppose you would never forget to pack a box of teabags in your suitcase. May I take some to the neighbour?'

'Have the whole box.' I pressed it into her hands, slightly aggressively because I was tired of feeling bad about the tinned pineapple. Luna was a lunatic. She screamed at the sight of peaches but loved blood and loved the Beatles. She added five spoons of sugar to her coffee and then knocked it back like a matador.

'If this dacha was made from chocolate,' she smiled, 'I could eat the whole house and never put on weight.' Her mother was always trying to get her to eat more than she needed because of the baby daughter who had not survived.

'But now, Saul, we are going to listen to the Beatles.' She pointed to a record player I hadn't noticed the last time I was here with Walter. It was perched on a chair at the end of the room, one side of it held together with beige tape. Luna had hidden her precious album, *Abbey Road*, in the kitchen drawer. It was wrapped in a towel, and when she unwrapped it, she gazed longingly at the cover and kissed John, Paul, Ringo and George in turn, and then kissed Ringo again. Twice. Three times. Quick tiny kisses.

'Is Ringo your favourite Beatle?'

'Yes. I like his nose. It's like your nose, Saul!'

She skipped over to the record player, and very carefully, as if she was holding something infinitely fragile and precious beyond measure, she slid the vinyl out of the cover. It was late afternoon and the sun was shining on Walter's allotment. So far there were no jaguars prowling around the plaster dwarves and gnomes that seemed popular amongst the dacha owners.

We listened to the whole of *Abbey Road*. Luna played 'Come Together' twice and 'She Came In Through the Bathroom Window' three times. We danced together and worked out some dumb but thrilling hand movements to make each other laugh. Meanwhile we were twisting our hips and shaking our heads in time with Ringo's drumbeat. I told her it made me feel nostalgic for London. 'Ah yes,' she said, 'I would like to see London. But most of all I want to go to Liverpool because I want to see Penny Lane for myself.'

While she was talking she unplaited her hair so that it fell to her waist. A baby jaguar could hide in it with ease. Luna was preparing to do something. She kicked off her black pointed Beatle boots and instructed me to find her a chair which I was to place in the middle of the room. I had to move the pile of old muddy boots I had tripped over last time, also the empty bottle of schnapps that Walter and I had polished off, also the matchbox containing my father's ashes, which for some reason I had put down on the floor next to the boots and forgotten to take with me. I slipped it into my jacket pocket.

'Look at me, Saul, look!'

Luna was standing on the chair with her arms stretched out, as if she were flying. She took a breath and, with her arms still outstretched, sang 'Penny Lane' from start to finish. She had a strong, high voice, and because she was singing the English words in a German accent, it was even more moving. When she sang one of the lines in German, her translation did not work that well.

'*Die schöne Krankenschwester verkauft Mohnblüten von ihrem Tablett.*'

I think it went something like: *The beautiful nurse is selling blossoms of poppies from her tray.* I did not tell Luna that a remembrance poppy was made from paper and that the poppies in the tray the nurse was holding symbolized the blood shed by wounded and dying soldiers on the fields of Flanders. While she was singing, I heard something growling. It wasn't nearby, it was far away, but I heard it all the same. It made me shiver while she sang. Luna jumped off the chair and bowed, her arms at her side, while I applauded.

'I know I will find work in a hospital in Liverpool.'

She told me that more than anything she wanted to be free.

'I am scared of everything' – she pointed to the clock ticking on the dacha wall – 'I can't see an end to it. I am frightened all the time. Morning to night and then it's morning again. When there is too much to feel, it is better to sing.' She apologized for making me feel worse about the pineapple. 'To be honest it is the syrup I crave more than the pineapple, but we are happy living with you here in the East. You have added something sweet to our lives. We are so glad to be your friends and we will miss you when you go. Do you want to see my ballet?'

'Yes.'

I was discovering that Luna liked to escape any way she could find.

She searched for her ballet shoes, which were lying under the table, their ribbons unlaced, as if she always offered to dance for the dacha guests. This time I was instructed to move three chairs, a basket containing two sticks of wilting rhubarb, a bag full of empty glass jars and to roll up a small rug.

Luna laced up her dusty ballet shoes with their strange solid toes, and for one hour in the late twentieth century in the German Democratic Republic showed me an art that began in the seventeenth century and was devised for the European courts to display the power and wealth of its rulers. There was longing and tenderness in the way she moved her arms, but her demeanour was reserved. She turned and whirled, two, three, six times, which she told me was her ballet teacher's special skill because she had trained the male dancers in the Bolshoi Ballet. Her body was ethereal and delicate as she finally plunged into a slow, steady, perfect arabesque *en pointe*.

*

Later, as she lay panting on the floor, I brought her a large glass of water and knelt down to untie the silk ribbons of her ballet shoes. She told me that if only I could dance too, we could try a *pas de deux*, which means 'steps for two'. With the support of someone else helping with the lifts and counterbalancing, she would be able to accomplish more than on her own. As the sun set over the dacha and the allotment, I locked the front door and unplugged the electrical devices, while Luna, still out of breath from her massive performance, told me more facts about the Beatles, as told to her by Rainer. She was particularly interested in how Paul and John had hitch-hiked out of Liverpool to Paris where their hair was cut by a barber called Jürgen, which was how their signature hairstyle came into being.

When I drew the curtains, I could see three iron girders thrusting out of the earth, perhaps left there after the war. The East had not benefited from the money that had been poured into the reconstruction of West Germany by America and its allies. Luna was still sitting on the floor. She grasped the heel of her bare right foot with her hand and turned it in circles as clouds shifted over the girders.

I was woken by the sound of a dog howling or perhaps a fox calling its cubs. When I sat up on the mattress that I had laid on the floor, I saw someone standing over me. A ghost, a spectre, shrouded in white cloth, its hair the colour of silver trees in a forest. Luna apologized for scaring me but told me it was clear to her that the jaguar was about to crash through the windows and pounce. She was scared it would drag her off somewhere bad, away from her ballet shoes and precious album, *Abbey Road*, away from her mother and brother, who would never recover; no one would know what had happened to her. And they would be too afraid to ask questions. I offered to turn on the lights and check the windows, but she did not think that would deter the jaguar. If anything the lights would encourage it to come closer. She climbed on to the mattress with me and lay on her side at some distance, as the dog continued to howl, or perhaps it was just whimpering. I felt her trembling. I lightly put my arm around her waist, chastely, careful to keep my body separate from hers. Yet something happened in the night. In our sleep we moved closer, until I was aware that my leg had entwined with hers and that her hand was stroking my arm. When she moved my hand to her breast I moved away from her, but she turned over so that she was facing me. It was she who made the next move, too. I should have resisted, but I did not, and then her white nightdress was lying somewhere on the floor. Nothing could have stopped us. It was easy because she was so turned on, it was all happening in erotic slow motion as if it had nothing to do with our own free will. Luna was all over me all the time, her lips pressed against my pearl necklace. I could see her eyes shining in the dark, and then it was over. The dog was still whimpering.

'Did Jennifer give you the pearls?'

I noticed that my hands were resting on my neck, as if protecting my pearls from her fingers. Most of all, I felt sad.

I had come to think that anything I might say about the pearls was an unfinished, endless conversation.

'Walter says your Jewish mother was born in Heidelberg and her father was a professor at the university.'

'I don't want to talk about it now.'

'But you must,' she said firmly. 'You are history.'

I closed my eyes and pretended to sleep.

It is possible the pearls were given to my mother by her mother when it became clear that at least the children must be helped to escape. Why would a child of eight own a pearl necklace when she arrived in Britain with her one suitcase? After she died, my father would give the pearls to his son because he did not have a daughter. And then how long would it take to explain that he did not expect his son to wear the pearls? They were supposed to be kept in a velvet-lined box and hidden in a drawer. I wore the pearls and they whispered non-stop, in German, every morning while my father and Matt ate their cornflakes.

I had been told by my friend Jack that Heidelberg was now home to a wild population of African rose-ringed parakeets. Both male and female parakeets are able to mimic human speech. That night in the dacha, I wondered what kinds of words they would have been mimicking after the pogrom called Kristallnacht.

The sun was rising over Walter's garden. I must have slept after all, because when I woke up I discovered more consciously that Luna and I were naked and tangled up in bed together.

'Let me see how long your hair is today, Saul.'

Her hands were in my hair, scooping it up and pulling it down, measuring its length in relation to my shoulders.

'Your hair is so black. Like the birds in the fields.'

I wanted her to go away. To leave me alone. To vanish.

'Luna, it's best to tell Walter we are just friends – is that all right with you?'

I felt her body stiffen.

'For breakfast I will cook us the mushrooms that you and Walter harvested.'

She was happy and affectionate while she set about frying the mushrooms.

It was odd to be sharing them with her and not with Walter. It was cold, and when I put on my jacket I remembered the matchbox of ashes I had placed in its pocket the night before. I asked Luna if she would mind if I buried my father's ashes in the garden. I showed her the matchbox. She was not shocked, if anything her expression was kind. She instantly agreed, slung on some trousers and a coat, which she wore over her white nightdress, and accompanied me to their family allotment.

I dug a small hole in the GDR with my hands, placed the matchbox of ashes into the hole and covered it with the soil that was my historical subject and torment. I felt bad that it was Luna's kind brother who'd had to fend off my questions.

Would you still have been my friend?

Luna stood by my side, bemused by this small personal ritual.

'I think you must have really loved your father.'

She walked back to the kitchen and left me alone with a sorrow so much bigger than the grave itself. I felt raw, as if I had just been disembowelled by a jaguar. A light breeze blew into the GDR, but I knew it came from America. A wind from another time. It brought with it the salt scent of seaweed and oysters. And wool. A child's knitted blanket. Folded over the back of a chair. Time and place all mixed up. Now. Then. There. Here.

I must have remained outside for a while, because when I returned, Luna was dressed and was now sawing through a loaf of heavy bread to take to the sick neighbour. I noticed she had embroidered the hems of her trousers.

'Do you make your own clothes, Luna?'

'Of course. All the trousers are ugly and when nice ones arrive in the shops they sell out in one afternoon.'

Even the dark bread seemed to be connected to the Beatles in Luna's mind.

'Rainer told me that John Lennon made his own bread when he got together with Yoko.'

She cut the loaf in half and then held the two halves against each other, to measure if they were equal. In her view, one half was not equal. She sawed through the loaf again, and then flinched. She had nicked the second finger of her right hand with the knife. Blood dripped on to the bread as she sucked her finger and then waved it in the air, above her head.

'I am a nurse,' she said.

'Yes, you told me.'

92

'But you didn't ask. I passed my exams with the best marks in my class. I want to take my studies further in the West and learn better English.'

'Walter can teach you English.' I moved the bread away from her bloody finger and suggested she rinse it in cold water.

'I want to train to be a doctor in Liverpool.'

'You can get good training here.'

She stamped her foot and turned to face me, her green eyes bright and clear.

'No. I need you to help me leave. I want to be free to travel and to study what I want. I am your girlfriend now.'

She moved towards me and kissed my left wrist, as if we were lovers, which I suppose we were.

'Listen, Luna.' I felt as if I were floating out of my body as I spoke. 'In September 1989, the Hungarian government will open the border for East German refugees wanting to flee to the West. Then the tide of people will be unstoppable. By November 1989, the borders will be open and within a year your two Germanys will become one.'

'You are lying to me.' She made her two fingers into a revolver and shot herself in the head.

'Bang. I love you. Rock and roll. You are my boyfriend.'

When she smiled with her snarled teeth, I truly felt that I was her prey.

'Tomorrow,' she said, 'I will make an emigration application to marry you and to live in the West.'

I knew that I must depart from the GDR as soon as possible. I would have to cancel my last two appointments with the librarian who had so reluctantly been helping me with the archives, and I would change my exit visa.

I began to think Luna was more dangerous than the jaguar she most feared. When she slipped her bloody finger under my pearl necklace and pulled it so the string was at breaking point, I lost my temper.

'I am in love with your brother.'

I felt her shock and rage. Luna picked up one of the pieces of sawn-off bread and threw it at me. It fell near my feet with a thump. I had betrayed her dream of leaving and I had betrayed her body because it was not the body I truly longed for. Yet it was she who had apparently offered her body to me freely. It was not free at all.

'Walter is married,' she said coldly. 'He has a wife and baby daughter.'

'Walter has a daughter?'

'Yes. Who do you think the little wooden train belongs to? My mother and I don't play with toys.'

She picked up the bread and wrapped it in a cloth.

'If I make an emigration application to marry you, then we can make an application for Walter to visit us because I am his sister.'

Two men were making a bonfire in a small field near the allotments. One of them was pouring a bag of leaves on to the flames. The other man poked the flames with a stick and then threw the stick into the fire.

'Do you want to live away from your friends and family?'

'Emigration is like that,' Luna said. 'Everyone knows this. Rainer knows this. He organizes transit vans with compartments under the seats. They are not stopped. If you don't want me to make an application you will have to pay him money to get me out.'

I told her I would think about it. She seemed to believe me and left the dacha to deliver the bread to her neighbour.

My head was throbbing. I closed my eyes and touched the ends of my hair. I was enraged to have been used in such a callous, cunning way. I walked over to the bashed-up record player held together with tape and lifted up the record that Luna had not put back in the drawer the night before. I threw *Abbey Road* to the floor and stamped with all my strength on the vinyl with my boots. It cracked and then shattered into four pieces, none of them equal.

*

I resolved to leave the GDR immediately. I would go back to the West, alone, without Luna, but I had to say goodbye to Walter first. Like a serious man would say goodbye to someone he cares for. No. I would not live apart from Walter. Not at all. I would discreetly speak to Rainer in the pub and ask him how much he charged for whenever Walter needed to leave. It was Walter's escape and not Luna's that was on my mind. I would free him from his life in hiding with his pretend wife.

14

There were at least nine women wheeling prams around the fountain in Alexanderplatz when I finally said goodbye to Walter Müller. Everywhere I looked there were women steering babies through the pigeons. It had been a sad and tense walk, but this time I carried my own bag. It seemed that Walter had suddenly stepped into his job as translator, just as I was leaving East Berlin. A copper relief sculpture on a tall building called the House of Travelling had caught my eye in Alexanderplatz. It was of an astronaut in a helmet setting off on his journey into the unknown, surrounded by various planets and birds and the sun. Walter translated its title for me.

'*Man Overcomes Space and Time*.'

'Yes,' I said, linking my arm with his, 'that's what I have been struggling with while I have been in the GDR. Space and time. But no way have I conquered it. In fact, it has conquered me.'

He squeezed my arm. 'No. You're just crazy. We look forward to your report on our economic miracle.' He threw back his head and laughed like a hound.

'No, Walter,' I said, 'you and I will soon meet for a beer in Kreuzberg.'

'When will that be, my English friend?'

'Whenever you decide.'

'Okay,' he replied. 'I would prefer to meet in Paris.'

'Then that's what we'll do.'

Walter stretched out his hand and messed up my hair. Although I was laughing, I was unhappy and scared, which made me wonder about Walter laughing all the time. Perhaps he was unhappy and scared, too.

The TV tower with its steel sphere and striped antenna was never out of view. Walter explained that it was designed to celebrate the Soviet obsession with space travel in the 1960s. 'Look at our World Clock,' he said in English. 'You will see on top of it a metal sculpture of the solar system.'

'Ah, asteroids and comets,' I said.

We were doing everything we could to avoid the moment we would both go our separate ways.

'Goodbye, Walter.' I said it very quickly with my eyes shut, and then I opened my eyes and saw all the women wheeling their children in prams. Perhaps the young woman in a yellow dress and white stilettos was his wife?

Walter stepped over my bag and held me fleetingly in his arms. I could smell the brown coal in his hair. He told me that while I was on the train heading back to the West, he would be helping out his friend who worked in a small kiosk at the end of his street. She sold sweets, drinks, cigarettes and newspapers. In the afternoon he was scheduled to teach English to men and women who had good careers but who were going to build socialism elsewhere, including Ethiopia. He seemed to want me to know what he would be doing while I was on the train to the West. And I did want to know. I wanted to know everything about Walter Müller. The fact that he had kept the details of his real domestic life hidden from me only made me love him more. He and I had both been very lonely in our teenage years in East Berlin and East London. I had suffered in the care of my authoritarian father and he had suffered in the care of his authoritarian fatherland.

'Please thank your mother for her hospitality.'

'I will do that,' he said. 'And thank you, Saul, for our conversations and for your company.' He shook my hand. 'Take care, Saul.'

'No,' I said, 'I want to take care of you.' And I meant it.

I leaned forward and whispered the information that Rainer had told me to relay to him. Walter flinched and stepped away from me. His face was pale.

'I grew up here. I would never leave for the West. I just want to see my aunt and cousins now and again.'

It began to rain on the World Clock and its metal solar system. The women wheeling prams were now running for cover. Everyone was running for cover.

Walter and I stood in the rain by the fountain with the pigeons while he told me in a low monotone that no one speaks their mind to Rainer. No one says anything to Rainer except good morning or goodnight. Why did I think Rainer had a brand-new three-roomed apartment? Why did he have a brand-new car when everyone else had to wait fifteen years? Why did I think Rainer was allowed to visit the West four times a year? Everyone knows not to talk to Rainer.

'Go back to your world,' he said sadly. And then he walked away from me and did not turn back. What he could not see when he stepped on to the road was that a van with the name of a furniture company written on its side had ignored the red traffic light. It pulled over and mounted the pavement to exactly where Walter stood waiting to cross the road. It was likely that he was going to be punished for attempting to flee from the republic and that it was my fault.

Abbey Road, London, June 2016

I stepped on to the crossing on Abbey Road, the famous zebra stripes, black and white, at which all vehicles must stop to make way for pedestrians. The Beatles crossed this same road in single file on 8 August 1969 for the record cover of *Abbey Road*. John Lennon leading in a white suit, George Harrison last in the line wearing blue denim, Ringo and Paul between them. A car was coming towards me but it did not stop. I fell on my hip, using my hands to protect myself from the fall. The car stalled and the driver rolled down the window. He was in his sixties, his eyelids quivering at the corners. He asked if I was injured. When I did not answer, he finally stepped out of his car.

'I apologize,' he said, 'but you stepped on to the crossing and I slowed down but then you changed your mind and then you stepped right in front of my car.'

I smiled at his careful and long-winded recollection of history told from his point of view.

'I'm all right, no problem.'

A catalogue for an exhibition of Jennifer Moreau's photographs had fallen out of my leather sling bag and, embarrassingly, so had a packet of condoms. I saw the driver was shocked; even his eyelids were quivering. He gazed at my right hand as blood dripped through my fingers. I sucked them while he watched me, clearly distressed, and then he asked if I needed a lift somewhere, or could he take me to a chemist? When I did not answer he asked for my name.

'It's Saul,' I said. 'Look, it's just a small cut. I have thin skin. I always bleed a lot, it's nothing.'

When I looked up I saw he was shaking, his knees were trembling.

I asked the driver for his name.

'Wolfgang,' he said quickly, as if he didn't want me to know.

He was holding his left arm with his right arm and his weird quivering eyes were crying blood. I wanted him to go away.

'My wing mirror is smashed,' he said. 'I bought it in Milan.'

He was moaning and seemed to be in pain.

'Can you tell me where you live? How old are you?'

When I told him I was twenty-eight he didn't believe me. I realized there was glass everywhere and that some of it was inside my head. I had gazed at my reflection in the wing mirror of his car and my reflection had fallen into me.

I was lying on the road. A mobile phone lay next to my hand. A male voice inside it was speaking angry and insulting words.

Fuck off I hate you don't come home.

My shoes were scattered on the road, too. Blue lights were flashing in my eyes. The man who was crying tears of blood told me it was an ambulance. As I was lifted on to a stretcher by two paramedics, I heard Luna's voice in my head. 'It is certain, Saul, that you have more than a gallon of blood in your body and the white blood cells will be fighting off infections.'

2

My father was eating a sandwich near my head. He tore off a piece of bread and rolled it into a ball.

'You're dead.'

'Not yet. It's you who's nearly dead.'

I could smell tinned mackerel on his breath.

'Where's your hawk?'

'Arthritis. Can't move my arm. I walk with a Zimmer now but I left it at home.'

'Are you Mrs Stechler?'

'I'm a mister, son, not a missus.'

I remembered that I was writing a paper on Stalin. His father, Beso, was a maniac. When Beso was young he was handsome and debonair. He could speak Russian, Turkish, Armenian and Georgian. When he died, aged fifty-five, he was buried in a pauper's grave. His son changed his name to Stalin, meaning 'man of steel', and went on to rule the Soviet Union.

'I'm in love with a man.'

Beso laughed in the Georgian manner. I waited for him to call my brother over to beat me. He was rummaging around for something.

'I've just returned from East Germany, the GDR. People want to travel and to be free.'

My father jabbed his finger somewhere near my face. 'These discontented intellectuals, capitalists and warmongers from the West should put a sock in it. They have no idea how bad conditions were for workers in the past or how the Russian people suffered. In the GDR no one was homeless, everyone had somewhere to live and no one was starving. That is why the state border had to be protected.'

He took out a plastic bag.

'It's your mother's necklace.'

I could move both my hands. I took the bag from him and brought them up close to my eyes. The pearls had last been touched by Luna's bloody finger.

'They cut it off when you were in surgery, but I've had it restrung for you. Glass in your inner organs. Sepsis. Ruptured spleen. Internal bleeding. They've attached a new silver clasp to the necklace. I would have paid for gold but they said the original was silver.'

'I wish I had given it to Luna. She liked my pearls.'

'Who's Luna?'

'My lover.'

'I thought you were in love with a man.'

'I am.'

I knew Jennifer Moreau was somewhere nearby because I could smell ylang-ylang.

I turned my head to look at her. She was wearing a hat and I could not see her face. I tried to move my hand to touch her hair. I held a strand in my fingers but it was not her hair because it was silver. I decided not to look at Jennifer again, but she could read my mind.

'You are in London.' Her voice had changed. It was deeper. She had a slight American accent.

I was not sure whether to believe her, because I could see Rainer walking towards me. He had swapped his khaki jacket for a white doctor's coat. The traitor had got rid of the guitar and replaced it with a stethoscope. By the time he got to my bed I knew what I wanted to say to him.

'You are not to be trusted. You live in a brand-new apartment with three bedrooms. You are a Stasi informer.'

'You might be right,' he replied, 'but it's not very likely.'

'Rainer is your doctor.' Jennifer uncrossed her legs and I could smell the sweet ylang-ylang.

'Listen, Jennifer, don't say anything to Rainer except goodnight and good morning.'

'Good morning, Rainer,' she said in her slightly American accent.

There was a machine near the bed. I was attached to it. Tubes were taped to the back of my hand.

I whispered to Jennifer, without looking at her.

'Did you get the flowers?'

'They are here,' she said, 'not roses, sunflowers.'

A vase of sunflowers stood on the table next to my bed.

'It's like this, Jennifer Moreau: I bought them for you.'

'It's like this, Saul Adler: I bought them for you.'

'Did you get my message, Jennifer?'

'What message?'

'From the careless man who loves you.'

'That was nearly thirty years ago.'

Rainer had disappeared.

As she leaned her face over my face, I shut my eyes. I was not ready to look at her. Her lips touched my forehead.

'Jennifer, are you really here?'

'Yes.'

'Where was I yesterday?'

'Here.'

'And the day before?'

Rainer came back. With another Stasi official in a white coat. I had seen him at a party in East Berlin and his name was Heiner. He was discussing the drip in my hand. They both said the same word my father had said. Sepsis.

Rainer disappeared again. Heiner followed him.

'Jennifer?'

'Yes, Saul.'

'I have to tell you something.'

'Go ahead.'

'I am in love with someone else. I am in deep with a man.'

'Who?'

'Walter Müller. I want to spend the rest of my life with him.'

'That's old news,' she said. 'That was when you were twenty-eight. By the way, I am in love with a man too.'

Someone else was by my bed.

My brother Fat Matt and his pinched-lipped wife. She reminded me that her name was Tessa.

'I'm glad you've come round,' she said, but I could tell she didn't mean it.

My brother Matt was leaning over my head.

'Keep your arms and hands outside the sheets. The tubes get tangled otherwise.'

'You fucking bastard,' I whispered to Fat Matt as he leaned in closer. His eyes were so big.

'I'm sorry about what happened, Saul. You've been flat-out.' A sound of a chair being dragged across a floor. To the edge. Of where I was now. Which was a bed. Next to a machine. I was attached to the machine with tubes. Matt reached for my hand.

I called for Rainer. 'You're good at making people disappear. Tell him to leave or you'll smash his fat face in.'

Rainer advised my brother not to take it personally.

'He is not entirely with us.'

I shut my eyes. It was the most basic magic to make him go away.

Take it personally, the voice in my head said loudly. It is personal.

When I opened my eyes again Matt was being led out of the room at a pace by his drab wife.

I pointed to my father.

'And him. He must go too.'

Rainer addressed my father as Mr Adler when he told him I needed to rest.

My head was very heavy when he said my father's surname so formally. It felt like someone was tapping it from the inside. *What does it make you think of?* It made me think of the plaited loaf of soft bread my mother baked on Friday mornings. A golden challah with sesame seeds. As a child I would beat the eggs and add the salt, sugar and oil while she poured in the frothing yeast and the flour. After we had left it for a few hours in the warm airing cupboard, we would begin my favourite task, which was to divide the dough into three pieces and plait them. When it was baked I would turn the loaf upside down and tap it to see if it was hollow. My mother made this bread for my father, who pretended not to care. But he did care because after she died he bought a challah every Friday. When I told him I knew how to make challah he said he didn't care. I saw Rainer leading my old man down the corridor. He had forgotten his walking stick and was limping.

Rainer came back. His stethoscope was somewhere on my chest. My heart. Cold. Cold. Cold Rainer. I asked him if he still read the beat poets.

'I don't know who they are.'

'But you smuggled in their books.'

'Did I now.'

'I suppose the authorities let you. They wanted the names of anyone reading them.'

He came up close to my ear.

'Where are you, Saul?'

'Germany. East. I swam in Honecker's personal lake.'

'Right,' he said. 'Germany East and West are together. The year is 2016. The month is June, the twenty-fourth. Yesterday Britain voted to leave the European Union.'

'You are despicable, Rainer,' I said. 'How old were you when the Stasi recruited you?'

I heard Jennifer coughing nearby.

'What did they do to Walter? What happened to Luna? Come on, Rainer. Answer my questions.'

'It's a good sign,' Rainer said, 'to be able to talk in full sentences and to order your family away from your bedside.'

'I can smell everything. It's too much. I know you have just eaten an apple, Rainer.'

His hands were on my stomach. He seemed to be attending to a bandage or looking at something under the bandage.

'You know, I have just eaten something like an apple. A dried apple ring my mother sent me from Dresden.'

'*Gebackene Apfelringe,*' I whispered.

'Wow,' Rainer said, 'you speak German?'

There must have been some sort of bandage on my head as well as my stomach because I could feel the tears slide underneath it.

'Rainer, I am very frightened for Walter. Will you give him a message for me? He's a translator. My lover.'

'I don't know who Walter is.'

'You do know. You have been given a passport to visit the West four times a year. You have a new car. Everyone else has to wait fifteen years to get one.'

'He's confused.' My father had returned and was looking for his stick. He was whispering with his mackerel breath, as usual embarrassed by his son's tears.

'I buried you in the GDR,' I whispered to the spectre called Mr Adler.

'If that is true, son, you will have buried your father alive.'

No one helped him find his stick. It hurt me to see him searching for it.

'Did you nail me into a coffin?'

'No, you were in a matchbox.'

My father seemed to have found his stick.

He was muttering something to Rainer about how it was his job

106

to bring his son back to reality and not to comply with his delusions. I could hear him explaining to my doctor, who might also be a Stasi informer, that I was a historian. My subject was communist Eastern Europe and somehow I had transported myself back to the GDR, a trip I had made when I was twenty-eight in the year 1988. Now, nearly thirty years later, while I was lying on my back in University College Hospital, I seemed to have gone back in time to that trip to the GDR in my youth. My father was always trying to bring me back to reality but I never much liked it there in the first place. I heard him breathing and grinding his teeth.

Once again, Rainer tactfully tried to get him to leave.

'We need Saul to be calm,' I heard him say.

'Are you banning me from seeing my own son?'

Rainer told him there were strict hospital visiting times.

'Piss off, doctor, your trains might run on time but we all know where they were going.'

'Yes,' Rainer said. 'I'm sorry. I don't believe in war myself.'

I started to like Rainer. Though I tried not to because of his treachery.

I began to mull over the problem of liking people we are not supposed to like, yet find ourselves becoming fond of them. A nurse was rubbing something cold into my arm. A needle pricked my skin. I opened my eyes. There was a woman visiting the patient in the bed next to me. She was holding a baby.

It hurt me to look at her child. I wanted her to take the baby away. Jennifer, who was close by, was looking at the baby too.

I called for Rainer. He had disappeared.

'What do you want?' Jennifer asked me.

'Take that baby away.'

'We can't do that,' she replied. 'But one day we must talk about America.'

I still couldn't look at her.

'What happened in America?'

She was silent.

'How old are you, Jennifer?'

'Fifty-one.'

'How old am I?'

'Fifty-six.'

'Where have we gone?'

'I am here. Where are you?'

'Alexanderplatz. Near the World Clock. I am standing with Walter.'

'Oh, right,' she said. 'That was a long time ago.'

'You never asked me.'

'Asked you about what, Saul?'

'If I minded.'

'Minded what?'

'Where's Rainer?'

'You're not his only patient, you know.'

'I need to know what happened to Luna.'

'Who is Luna?'

'Walter's sister.'

'Here's Rainer.' She waved to the doctor and walked towards him. I saw his hand touch the back of her hand. I did not believe I was fifty-six. But I could believe Jennifer was fifty-one, even though I had not looked at her face. She was plumper and wealthier, her clothes, her shoes. The man lying in the bed next to me had asked for her autograph. She signed the plaster cast on his left leg as if she were famous, but that might have been something people do on plaster casts anyway. Except that when she drew a goat or something like that with her pen, he said he would have to keep the cast after they cut it off because her drawing was worth more than his flat. Her dress was made from something flimsy with tiny polka dots all over it, a dress that younger Jennifer would never have worn.

Later he showed me what she had written.

Get a leg over

J. M.

'How do you know Jennifer Moreau?'

'She's my girlfriend.'

He laughed and then stopped himself.

'There's a man who stands by your bed at night. He says his name is Wolfgang. He wants to talk to you but you're always asleep when he arrives.'

3

In the wakefulness of the long nights in hospital with its nocturnal moaning and whispering, I thought about the astronaut on the tall building in East Berlin, whirling through space and time with the planets and the birds.

Yet here on the Euston Road, I was not in GDR time and space, I was floating somewhere above America. I could hear the sound of waves crashing on the sand slopes of a beach called Marconi while office workers in London drank beer in pubs and film executives filled the local tapas bars. As patients snored or cried out for help, an ocean flowed through the twilit ward of the hospital. Outside, a truck pulled up to collect the rubbish bags off the London streets while I stood alone on Marconi Beach. There were seals in that ocean. A lighthouse nearby. It was an anguished space. I wanted to move elsewhere, with the gulls and the planets. And I did move on, but not very far, perhaps just a few miles down the coast. There are ponds and clapboard houses and shacks selling lobster. Jennifer is walking down a sandy path by the salt marshlands near a coastal place called Wellfleet, New England. She is lying on her stomach amongst the tall reeds and she is inconsolable. At sunrise Jennifer leans and weeps against the door of a clapboard house. I know she has used up all her strength on whatever it is that lies behind the door. There is a cherry tree in the garden. When the wind blows, its blossom falls through the universe like pink rain.

*

I was aware that sometimes in the afternoon, the man who ran me over was standing by my bed, a spectre of judgement and blame. I recognized his weird quivering eyes. I knew he was ashamed and that it was something to do with the object I had found on the road.

'Go away, Wolfgang,' I whispered. 'Make sure your brakes work this time.'

He was in the mood for talking, even though I was not available to him. He even made small talk about Christmas. He told me his parents came from Austria, a place called Spitz in the district of Wachau, a ninety-minute drive from Vienna airport. The wine-producing district. Grapevines. The Danube. Small villages. A monastery. He and his husband bought all their Christmas decorations from Spitz, including the chocolate liqueurs filled with kirsch to hang on their tree. They had found a straw goat at a fair and decorated it with grapes, which would dry into raisins. He had an adopted brother who was from Bucharest but now lived in Zurich.

'You have a husband?'

'I do, yes.'

Apparently, City airport had been closed that morning because an unexploded bomb from the Second World War had been found in the Thames. He could no longer drive so he had taken a train and a tube to find me. Warren Street tube station was nearby. It was on the Victoria Line, represented on the tube map as the light blue line. That kind of blue was too cheerful for me, but no one knew that, except Wolfgang. I reached out my hand to catch the blossom falling from America.

4

Rainer was always the guardian angel when my father and brother came to visit me. He courteously saw them off, insisted they stay away. As far as he was concerned their presence was interfering with my recovery. Rainer was born in Dresden, once called the Florence of the Elbe. Yes, Rainer was born near the Czech border. I wondered if he had heard of the cakes that Walter liked in Prague called little coffins?

'No, I don't think I ever saw a little coffin.'

'You know, Rainer, I wish you had been around when I was young and growing up.' He encouraged me to sleep. A few minutes after he left, I heard a mirror shatter. It was an echo of something that had happened on the Abbey Road crossing. I had glanced at myself in the wing mirror of the car, Wolfgang's car, and it had exploded into a heap of reflective shards. Some of them were inside my head.

The nights were all about phantoms in America. In the day, lying on my back in the hospital on the Euston Road, I was usually somewhere in the GDR.

I could smell the glue in Ursula's apartment in East Berlin. It was made from the bones of animals. Walter had used it to mend the wooden train with red wheels.

'The lights are very bright here,' I said to Rainer. 'They are not like moonlight, which is the earth's nightlight.'

'Correct,' Rainer said encouragingly.

'They are like interrogation lights.'

'Have you ever been interrogated, Saul?'

'No. But Walter has and it's my fault.' I was sweating. I sweated all night and all day and was convinced it had more to do with fear than sepsis.

'It's good to hear you talking again.' Rainer adjusted the drip that was inserted into the back of my hand. 'Even though you speak of sad events from another time. Is it true that your friend would have been interrogated?'

'I think it is likely to be true.'

Rainer nodded as if he agreed it was likely to be true, which made me feel worse.

'I want you to get stronger and to lead a normal life.'

'What is a normal life, Rainer?'

'In medical terms I can answer that, sort of. But I don't think that is what you mean to ask me.'

I wondered if he had been speaking to Wolfgang.

'You know you are very fortunate? You ruptured your spleen. Internal bleeding. Not too bad, considering.'

'What is a spleen?'

'An organ in the upper far left of the abdomen, to the left of the stomach. It's shaped like a fist, about four inches long. The surgeon has removed part of your spleen, not the whole thing. She wanted to avoid the risk of infection but it's got infected anyway.'

The Stasi officials disguised as doctors were also taking scans of my brain. The images were sent to the radiologist, who wrote reports for Rainer to read. There were people looking at detailed images of the inside of my head. When I asked Rainer, again, how it was that he became an informer, he dragged a chair to the right side of my bed and moved his face closer to my right ear, which is where I could best hear him. It meant he had to talk to me in a strange position, his lips near my ear. I appreciated him making the effort. He wanted me to understand that it was important to get some facts straight. He was a doctor, not a Stasi spy. We were in Britain in 2016.

'But when did I cross Abbey Road?'

'You have crossed Abbey Road many times,' Jennifer interrupted. Sometimes I forgot she was there.

'Why did I cross Abbey Road so many times?'

'To have sex with me of course.'

'But when did I get run over?'

'Ten days ago.'

'I've mixed then and now all up.' My words came out slurred, as if I were drunk.

'That's what I do in my photographs.' Jennifer put on her coat and tapped my nose with what she thought was affection, but it hurt.

Rainer seemed to be reliable and kind. It was hard to believe that he could be trusted. It was all the more confusing because he was from Germany, which is where he trained at medical school. I wasn't going to let him off lightly.

'Did you inform on the priest and the people in your church group, Rainer?'

'Nope.'

'You were not alone. There were eighty-five thousand full-time employees of the Stasi and sixty thousand unofficial collaborators, one hundred and ten thousand regular informers and half a million part-time informers.'

Rainer clapped his hands as if he were applauding an opera.

'Saul,' he said, 'your brain is switched on again.'

I was shocked to hear it was ever switched off. I explained that I was a historian. I wondered if my students were waiting for me to unlock the lecture theatre and indeed give a lecture.

'I think your brother is sorting out your sick leave at the university.'

'So long as he's not teaching my students.' I must have smiled because the corners of my mouth had turned upward.

Rainer told me he knew of an informer in the GDR who had reported a colleague who had had too many beers and criticized the educational policies. These were stories that people knew about. But my question about what a normal life might be interested him. He thought we should leave out the medical aspect and try to figure out the rest of it.

'Tell me, Saul, what do you think a normal life would be like?'

He started to answer his own question. Housing. Food. Work. Health.

'Those things were not enough for Luna.'

I was crying and sweating. What was the rest of it? To live without fear. No, that was impossible. To live with less fear, I whispered to Luna. To live with more hope. To not be hopeless all the time. I didn't know where all the tears were coming from. Life is shocking. But the shock seemed to go back a long time to my mother's car crash. To America. To East Berlin. And then forwards and backwards and all over the place to missing Walter Müller. Maybe a normal life was sitting in a pub with Walter and having a beer. I still couldn't think about being fifty-six. I had not seen my face in a mirror since the accident. The mirror was inside me. Jennifer had returned to my side. She was eating cheese. Salty goat's cheese. I think she had given some of it to Rainer. He was holding a paper napkin in his hand. Did doctors eat lunch on the ward? I was still suspicious of Rainer.

After a while I told them both that I would like to see my mother again.

'Then perhaps you should visit her.' Jennifer was now wiping her fingers on the napkin she had passed to Rainer.

'She's dead.'

I lifted my fingers to my head.

'Jennifer, where is my hair?'

'Don't think about it. Visit your mother.'

It was our old game. We had played it many times when we still loved each other. Jennifer was wearing a black silk shirt. A pencil poked out of its pocket. I could smell the leather of her bag when she took a notebook out of it. Leather and silk. This was older Jennifer. The goat's cheese was more like younger Jennifer, when she was a vegetarian and made sweet potato curry with Saanvi and discussed infinity in the sauna for hours while Claudia practised her t'ai chi positions.

The pencil was now gripped in her fingers.

'I can see cobblestones and a castle,' I said.

'That doesn't sound like Bethnal Green.'

'Heidelberg. A Gothic university on a hill surrounded by forest.'

Her hand did not move across the page that lay open on her lap.

'It is one of the world's oldest surviving universities.'

Her hand was soft and still. I wanted to kiss it but I feared she might walk away.

'I thought you were going to draw?'

'I don't like drawing buildings,' she said. 'So far, we have never met your mother.'

I touched my head again. And then again.

'Jennifer, am I ugly now?' She did not answer and I still couldn't look at her, but I knew she was the real Jennifer because of the ylang-ylang that always came with her. Rainer was sitting on the visitor's chair next to new older Jennifer, whose older fingers gripped the pencil, waiting for me to say something that interested her. I glanced at her feet. She was wearing silver shoes with three silver straps buck-led across the instep. The toe of her right shoe rested on the toe of Rainer's black polished shoe.

I heard myself speaking for Jennifer's pencil, anything to get the toe of her sandal away from Rainer's shoe.

I am walking on the cobblestones of the main drag in Heidelberg. A man has laid out a blanket on the stones. He sits on the blanket, play-ing his guitar. Three dogs sleep at his feet. His guitar seems to attract other dogs from the town: I can see them making their way to the blanket. He's only playing three chords, but they like it. They shut their eyes, calmed by his very basic music.

'I like basic music too.' Jennifer sounded quite cheerful so I must have stopped boring her. Why was she always by my side?

Please, I say to the man playing his guitar, can you tell me where I can find my mother? He shakes his head and requests in a whisper that I do not bring my own sadness to Germany and wake up the dogs.

'Jennifer, where is my hair?'

I could see her hand moving across the page. It was such hard work being involved with someone like Jennifer Moreau. I was even obliged to entertain her from my sickbed.

'At least we've got past the butcher's shop in Bethnal Green,' she said.

I glanced at her sketchbook. Jennifer had drawn the man with the dogs sleeping by his feet. She had written in pencil, 'Let sleeping dogs lie.' Except one of the dogs had its eyes open.

My eyes were open too. Jennifer's silver shoe had now fallen off her right foot. Someone must have undone the three buckles of the straps.

Rainer had disappeared. He lived in an office somewhere in the wall.

'But you didn't meet your mother.' Jennifer ripped the page out of her sketchbook.

'Oh God, Jennifer, is it true that you were pregnant when I returned from East Berlin?'

She slid the pencil back into the pocket of her black silk shirt. 'Shall we talk about what happened when you got back from the GDR?'

'Yes, I want to. Anything to get away from the sleeping dogs in Heidelberg.'

5

In late January 1989, Jennifer and I were sitting in a cheap Italian restaurant called Pollo in Old Compton Street, Soho. It was always full of students from St Martins art school around the corner because it offered its loyal impoverished customers three courses for a fiver. Jennifer had introduced me to Pollo when we first met. Once we discovered spaghetti vongole and penne arrabbiata it felt like we had one toe in the Mediterranean, even though it was January and our fingers were numb under our gloves. Jennifer was pregnant and she said the child was mine. This was the first time we had seen each other since I had returned from East Berlin. She said she wanted to keep the child, despite graduating from art school with a first-class degree. She was leaving Britain to take up her residency in America. I had not realized how large her belly would be at four months pregnant. Perhaps it was relative because she was usually as slim as a pencil. Despite the cold, she wore a pale yellow halter-neck dress under a thick cardigan because nothing else fitted her. She devoured a plate of spaghetti bolognese even though she was supposed to be a vegetarian. While she drank water, I knocked back a carafe of red wine and then ordered another one.

'It's like this, Saul Adler: we have separated so I will bring up my child without you.'

'It's like this, Jennifer Moreau: I am happy to abolish all traditions. I am with the poets and heretics and dissidents. It's your body and you do what you wish with it.'

That was a shock tactic because what I wanted was for Jennifer to marry me and for us to live together and to raise our child together, but I thought she would reject me (again) if I spoke my wish out loud. Instead I asked if she would like to borrow my jacket.

'I'm not cold.'

It was true that it was warm inside Pollo. Everyone was smoking and shouting as the waiters thumped plates of steaming pasta on the Formica tables. A young man with a blue Mohican was stubbing his cigarette out in the avocado that had arrived on a plate. It was stuffed with something pink.

'That's Otto,' Jennifer whispered. 'He's a genius and he taught me a lot.' Otto looked about fifteen but Jennifer said he was twenty-three. She waved to him. He waved back and pointed contemptuously at his prawn cocktail.

'Chef wanted!' he shouted across the tables.

She told me that Otto was going to help her carry her suitcase to the airport in ten days' time.

'Don't go, please don't go, but if you do I will help you with your bags. You haven't given me your address or your telephone number.'

It was as if she hadn't heard me.

After a while, she asked me to tell her about my stay in the GDR.

She was not that surprised when I told her about my affair with Walter Müller. She listened for a long time. While I was speaking, a woman waiting with a crowd of students for a table to become free spilled the glass of wine that Otto had passed to her on to Jennifer's yellow halter-neck dress. This accident prompted me to tell her about spilling coffee on Walter's only pair of Wrangler's.

'He sounds like an interesting person. How did he fit into your jeans?'

'With difficulty.'

'What do you think of him having a wife and child?'

'He has to live a double life.'

'Do you live a double life?'

'No.' I dabbed at the wine stain on her yellow dress with a napkin. 'I have always been open with you about my sexuality.'

I did not tell her about Luna.

It was a crisp, cold winter evening in Soho. We were angry and confused but we could not stop touching each other. We walked down Frith Street and when I put my arm around her shoulders I noticed that after a while her arm slipped around my waist. She was twenty-four and pregnant. Her lips were soft as she shivered, despite the chunky cardigan that Saanvi had knitted her. This time I did not ask her permission, I took off my jacket and draped it over her shoulders.

'You know, Saul, you might be a good father.' Suddenly we were kissing outside Ronnie Scott's. Deep kissing. In that kiss I tried to beam all my love into her. My eyes were open and hers were closed, her eyelashes mascaraed blue. I noticed she had pierced her nose in the months since we had separated. I couldn't believe I had not seen the small gold hoop glittering in her right nostril when we sitting together at Pollo.

'You are blooming,' I said to her. 'Your hair and eyes are shining and your breasts have become heavier.'

'I told you never to describe my body to me or to anyone else.'

I had hoped that the pregnancy would free me from our agreement, but apparently it had not.

We kissed again and when I looked down there was a beggar, a man sitting on the pavement with his dog. He was about thirty. A year older than myself. He caught my eye and gave me the thumbs up. When I placed my hand on Jennifer's stomach, she pushed it away. We continued kissing.

'I will be a good father,' I whispered in her cold ear.

'Yes. But you would be a terrible husband.'

'We don't have to get married.'

'You're already a terrible boyfriend.'

When I told her I loved her and wanted to be with her when the baby was born, she suddenly raised her hand.

I thought she was going to push me into the gutter with the beggar, but she was hailing a taxi.

'Yes,' older Jennifer said, 'I knew I had to get away from your love as fast as possible.'

Her shoes were lying somewhere on the floor.

'I don't think either of us had a clue.'

'Very likely,' she agreed, but she was on her phone. Her voice was unrecognizable to me, perhaps because she was speaking to someone she loved. 'Sweetheart, if you've lost your Travelcard, it might be with your keys. Look in all your pockets.'

After she'd put her phone away, I asked her if she would like me to do up the buckles on her shoe. Jennifer scooped the silver shoes up and swung her feet on to the bed while I attempted to do something normal like fasten a buckle. It was a very tricky task to perform with a drip in my arm.

'It's not that I didn't want your love,' she said suddenly, 'it's more like I didn't feel it.'

'That's not true,' I whispered, 'I know you felt it.'

'True. It was more like I wanted all your love, but that was never going to happen.'

I remembered the portrait of myself on her bedroom wall. How she had outlined my lips in red felt-tip, three words graffitied underneath it.

DON'T KISS ME.

'You made off with my son,' I reminded her, trying and failing to ease the spike of the buckle into the leather hole.

'You were in love with Walter Müller.'

A nurse was doing the rounds in the ward. The sound of a plastic curtain whooshing around the beds. Whispered questions and answers. Sometimes moans of pain or stoic laughter.

'It's like this, Jennifer Moreau: you took our son off to live in America.'

'It's like this, Saul Adler: that's where the work was. It was the start of everything. I had just graduated. How was I going to support my child?'

'You could have asked me.'

'You should have offered.'

'Was I there at the birth?'

'No.'

Her right shoe was now more or less buckled, three silver straps across her ankle.

'Our son's name is Isaac. Is that right?'

'Yes.'

I turned my back on her and pulled the white sheet over my head.

Her phone began to ring again. Something about the caller having found the keys but not the Travelcard. Jennifer was laughing but she sounded desperate. ' Darling, why don't you ask your father?' I had no idea what was going on. It was the sort of love I knew nothing about. I touched my ears as if to close all portals to the sort of love I heard in Jennifer's voice.

6

One of the spectres that came to haunt me on the Euston Road was Luna Müller. She had no physical form, but I could feel that she was nearby. Maybe she was scared of wolves and jaguars and needed company. Luna was always slightly breathless, as if she was dancing, or perhaps running. I wondered if she had come to tell me she had made it to Liverpool. Had she discovered that Penny Lane was in the part of the city known as Mossley Hill, which is where John and Paul grew up? Or that Penny Lane was named after James Penny, a merchant and slave-ship owner who defended the slave trade to the British parliament? What did Luna from the GDR think about that then?

She did not reply and I began to worry about how she was always out of breath. All the same, it was comforting to sometimes feel her near me. Despite the way we had parted, I felt endeared to her, but I didn't want to think about that. I couldn't stop thinking about that. I said it out loud, 'I feel endeared to her.' I tried to attach myself to the man who was saying that but I wasn't sure it was really myself. It made a change from the other spectre, namely Wolfgang, but I was too tired to open my eyes for him. I preferred the images behind my eyes, especially of Luna, her lustrous hair coiled around her head. She looked like a swan. A swan on the Spree. Her breasts and hips were heavier in the new memories that I was making of her.

*

One night when I was with Luna, I made the mistake of opening my mind to Wolfgang. His white shirt was ironed and starched, the collar pinned with a single blue topaz in the shape of a rose. Perhaps it was blue because I was looking at it. I was black and blue all over. My hair was black and I was blue inside.

He was there to give me some information to do with Luna. His lips were thin and dry and he licked them while he spoke.

'They say you are no longer unconscious, but I'm not so sure. Your head hit the silver cat on the bonnet of my Jaguar.'

I wanted him to leave. Luna would have agreed with me. She wanted to escape from a reality that was so rational it was a little bit mad. My brother and father were insanely rational. They liked pointing their manly fingers in judgement. At me. As if they always knew what they meant. As if they always knew why and what and how. As if they always talked straight. As if their thoughts never bent out of shape. The man who ran me over began to tell me about his car. Apparently, it was a vintage E-Type Jaguar, first shown to the world in Geneva in 1961. The seats were made from marbled doeskin leather. He had bought the wing mirrors in Milan. The steering wheel had been carved from wood. He was most proud of sourcing the jumping Jaguar hood ornament. It had not originally been fitted to the E-Type, but alas, it was no longer in one piece.

I closed my mind and saw him off. All the same, I knew he would return because I did not want him to. Some of the shards of his wing mirrors bought in Milan were inside me. I was connected to the Jaguar. It was in my head, which was bandaged.

I had been given a plastic bowl of tinned pineapple by the woman who wheeled the lunch trolley. I saved it for Luna.

The nurse on the night shift didn't seem to mind me talking to her about the nurse I had met in the GDR in 1988. I told her how Katrin Müller wanted to see Penny Lane for herself.

'Was she your girlfriend?'

'No.'

'But you talk about her a lot.'

'I'm worried about her. She has a treacherous friend who offered her the chance to escape.'

'What do you think happened to her?'

'I don't know. She was scared of wolves and jaguars. Luna is short for lunatic.' I started to cry. 'She was frightened all the time. She couldn't see an end to it.'

A fragment of a poem I did not know I knew came to mind. I spoke it out loud to the night nurse.

'We are the Dead. Short days ago,
We lived, felt dawn, saw sunset glow,
Loved and were loved . . .'

She nodded as if I was being normal, which I wasn't.

'It's by John McCrae,' I said. 'He was a Canadian doctor but he signed up as a gunner in the First World War.'

The night nurse told me I was making progress. I asked her if I would be home soon. She couldn't tell me, but in her view, probably when I was able to walk and boil a kettle without help from anyone else. On one of the occasions she brought me a cup of tea 'out of hours' and asked about Jennifer. I noticed for the first time that her accent was Irish. She stuck a thermometer in my mouth while the plastic cup of tea cooled on the table by my bed.

'Do you know your ex is always at your side? We're all talking about it.'

She was silent and attentive while she took my pulse.

I pulled the thermometer from my mouth. 'She's not my ex.'

'Oh. Well then, sorry, but she told me she was your girlfriend in the past.'

'We are very much in love.'

'Is that right?' She put the thermometer back in my mouth. 'Your ex wears a very strong fragrance.'

I pulled the thermometer from my mouth again. 'Ylang-ylang.'

'Can you stop doing that?'

She plucked the thermometer from my fingers and told me the sepsis was more or less conquered. The bowl of pineapple stood near the cup of tea. A thin green mould was creeping over the chunks.

'Shall I chuck that away for you?'

I shook my head.

'You have such blue eyes, like my Siamese. Goodnight, Saul.'

The way she said goodnight. As if she did not expect to see me in the morning.

7

Two of my female colleagues at the university had made the effort to visit the Euston Road. I was touched they thought I was worth the long journey from East Berlin. They still seemed to have a low opinion of me. I either spoke too loudly or too softly or too fast or not fast enough. This time my eyes were not Oceanic.

I thanked them for their help researching the youth movements that had begun in the Rhineland as an alternative to the culture of the Hitler Youth. My colleagues told me they were from the university near Hendon, North-west London. It was close to the North Circular and A41, but Central London was only a thirty-minute journey on the Thameslink rail line and Northern Line. The university was committed to a green transport policy so they had travelled on the train.

My students had signed a card and had a whip-round to buy me a bunch of roses from the Asda on the Edgware Road. The card was of Lenin unfurling the mighty red flag. Someone had drawn a pearl necklace around his neck with a black felt-tip. My colleagues told me about the new vice chancellor at another university somewhere in England. Apparently, he employed a fleet of staff to bring his Coke and sushi to his office on a tray. Three white lace doilies were to be placed on the tray, one for the glass of iced water, one for the plate of fruit, usually grapes and pears, one for the extra glass for his Coke. At teatime, around four in the afternoon, his preference, in addition to a pot of Earl Grey, was for an assortment of Scottish shortbread biscuits, Italian hazelnut biscuits, English biscuits sandwiched together with raspberry jam, an almond-filled finger of sponge tipped with chocolate (no one had heard of it before he arrived, but apparently it was called a Gazelle Horn) and one single brandy snap served with vanilla cream. It was the tea tray that compensated for the austerity of his lunch and most panicked his staff. He owned a private helicopter, they joked, and a summer dacha near Bath Spa which he bought from a Russian oligarch. Many of the academic staff were applying for the more secure job of bringing him his Coke and sushi, but wondered if they should ask for a pay rise to prepare the tea tray. Their humour was similar to the jokes I had heard in East Germany.

After they left I threw the roses in the bin.

Someone took the roses out of the bin.

To my horror it seemed that my father was a kind man. He left small gifts by the side of my bed. A flask of soup. He had made it himself. The leeks and potatoes were so crudely chopped I couldn't get any of the liquid out of the flask. One day he left a box of fudge called Cornish Clotted Cream. I held the box in my hands and understood he had remembered it was a childhood favourite. It made me feel faint to hold it. I drifted off and it fell from my hand.

Rainer told me it was hard for my elderly father to make the journey to the hospital, but I didn't want to see him. Or Matt. All the same, Rainer must have relented and allowed them to visit at certain times. His teeth were very straight and white, not at all British, perhaps more German. I couldn't tell Matt that I had attempted to visit our mother in Heidelberg, because he would mock me for making that kind of journey in the first place. Rainer advised me to give my father a chance, but I did not want to see him. I felt betrayed that he let my father hobble into the ward at various times. Although Rainer was a traitor, he too was so very kind. Like Walter.

I lay on my pillows thinking about the kindness of men.

I was being treated like a child by men who were infinitely gentle, yet

I was nearly sixty. What had happened between thirty and fifty-six? Those years were lost to morphine. Matt brought in a black-and-white photograph. It was of 'us boys' sitting on a pair of swings in the yard of our Bethnal Green home. I was twelve, he was ten. His hair was blond, mine black. He was called Matthew because that was the name of my father's best friend at junior school. This friend had come from a Quaker family. According to my father, Matthew's family were his 'extra' family because they believed in the values of social solidarity and human dignity. They enriched his life. Matthew's mother had taught my father how to read, and, oddly, how to make lemon curd. I think this extra accomplishment, learned from his extra family, made my father feel suave. He made lemon curd all through our childhood. We used to like watching him scrape off the lemon rind with a carrot peeler. My brother, Fat Matt, also called Matty by our mother, had a lot to live up to. Social solidarity and human dignity, just for starters. In the photograph we were both smiling, but we didn't mean it. Our mother had just died. There was a spectre haunting our house in Bethnal Green, lurking in the kitchen amongst the rotting eggs and chicken bones.

'You looked like a beautiful girl,' Matt said. 'Look at your long eyelashes.'

I drifted off, only to discover my father was there too.

'Dad made those swings for us.'

I glanced again at the photograph of the swings that Matt was so shamelessly holding under my eyes.

The swings were swinging back and forth. Our shoes dragging on the ground. The back door to the house in Bethnal Green was open. Soon we would have to go inside. Our mother's clothes were still in the wardrobe. A pair of her shoes lay under the kitchen table. I was wearing her pearl necklace under my T-shirt. Matt jumped off his swing. And then he pushed me on my swing until I was flying high in the air. He started to shout like a maniac, wanting me to jump off the swing while I was six feet in the air. I would not jump. I would not get off that swing. I would not walk into that house. Jump. Jump. Jump. His red face. His dead eyes. His screaming mouth. His big hands. Jump. Jump.

My father walked into the yard. His shoulders were bent. His hair unbrushed. His hands covered in dried plaster. He had been working all day with his hawk and his trowel. Matt kicked the backs of my legs every time the swing swung his way. My legs were thin and delicate and he hated them. At the same time, he pushed the swing with such force it was coming off its hinges. Jump. Jump. My father just watched him. He was not vigilant on my behalf, but he was aggressive in his passivity amongst the pots of geraniums and daffodils. My father stared into the distance while my brother kicked and pushed me at the same time. He reminded me of the guard near the lake in the GDR. The man who stood on the wooden platform in a tree, passive in his aggressive vigilance on behalf of the regime. Jump. Jump. It might be that I would have to jump to save myself from the swing that was about to crash to the ground. In the end the neighbour had to intervene. She knew we had just lost our mother and my father had lost his wife. She pulled Matt away from the swing. He fought her but she held him down, while my father watched in silence. I got off my swing and ran into the house where my mother was no longer there to see off my predators, the men who were mortified by my freakish beauty. Was I one of them or what? My brother saved his revenge for later.

I turned to Matt.

'Where was I when I was forty?'

He thought about this for a while.

'We never saw much of you. Sometimes you sent us a postcard from your holidays.'

'Yes,' my father wheezed, 'you liked the pastries in Lisbon and the museums in Paris.'

Matt took over. 'You sent us a postcard of Van Gogh's starry night when you were in Arles with Claudia.'

I looked to my side to see if Jennifer was there. To my relief the only sign that she had been at my side was the torn-out page of her drawing of the sleeping dogs in Heidelberg. Except all the dogs had their eyes wide open.

My father and brother began to name the countries I had visited. Matt collected the stamps from the postcards I had sent him. He had two children to support and spent all his money doing up their home in Britain. His favourite stamp was from Bombay, but he liked the Greek stamps too. I knew they were trying desperately hard to avoid mentioning the postcard I had sent them from Cape Cod, Massachusetts.

'And then you got a bit of a paunch,' Matt said. 'You spent more time in your cottage in Suffolk and started to grow two kinds of tomatoes.'

I waggled my fingers at him.

'Three.'

'Yes,' Matt said. 'The usual plum, then San Marzano and the big ones, here goes, Cost-ol-uto Fior-ent-ino.'

I could hear my father guffawing. 'Yes, those ones. You were always the bourgeois in the family and Matt the Bolshevik.'

They were still working hard to avoid arriving in Cape Cod.

My father tapped his false teeth.

'And then there is Jack, of course.'

I lifted my arm over my eyes. Where was Jack? There were so many people around me, making sure I did not slip out of this world. Jack would understand that no one had asked for my own opinion on this endeavour.

My father lowered his voice.

'Son, you mentioned you buried me in a matchbox.'

I nodded.

'I think you were remembering a very small coffin.'

His old hand reached for my hand and he squeezed it.

We had finally arrived in Cape Cod, Massachusetts.

After a while my brother led my father away.

8

Although I peeped now and again at Jennifer, I did not really look at her. There was something painful to find out, but I was in enough pain already. I had been moved to a private room, away from the anguished howls of elderly demented patients. My own howling kept me awake all night, anyway. Jennifer was at my side in my new private room. A new bunch of sunflowers stood tall in a vase at the foot of my bed. I was wearing my own clothes now, but I still had not looked in a mirror. Jennifer lifted off her hat. I could smell the ylang-ylang and knew she wished to smell like a flower for Rainer and not for me. She was reading a book by my side.

I made a decision to look at Jennifer. I am not sure what it was that I wanted to find out. I have done a lot of sly looking at women, of course, and my mother is frozen in my mind at the age she died, and I have been given a great deal of attention by women, but I have never said to myself, now you are going to look at a woman. Especially a woman I was forbidden to describe.

'Show me your face, Jennifer.'

'This is my face.'

When I at last looked at Jennifer I gasped and hid my head under the sheets. She did have another face. It was sadder and softer. Lines under her eyes and around her lips. Her angular face had changed to something plumper. Two silver hairs sprouted from her chin.

You are not Jennifer, I whispered into the pillow. The spectre of ylang-ylang lingered in the air. When I lifted my own hand to my eyes, I looked at it for a long time and saw that it too was not a hand I recognized. When I placed it on my stomach, which was stitched and bandaged, I encountered folds of flesh where it had once been flat. My stomach had turned into a belly. I wanted to catch up with my body. I moved my new older hand under my pyjamas and touched my penis, which seemed to be recognizable, as were my testicles. My pubic hair felt familiar, too. I moved my hand to my chest and felt hair that was soft and pleasing. I touched my nipples, the left and the right, and then I shut my eyes.

'Jennifer?'

'Yes?'

'Tell me again how old you are?'

'Fifty-one.'

'How old am I?'

'Fifty-six.'

I lifted the sheet from my head and stared into her eyes that were no longer the eyes of the woman I used to know. All her beauty that I was not allowed to describe, blown to bits in space and time.

She was still reading her book.

'What happened to our youth, Jennifer?'

I heard her turning the pages.

'That's a good question, Saul. How old do you think you are?'

'Twenty-eight.'

'That was your age when we were together.'

'What was I doing then?'

'You were getting ready to go to East Berlin.'

'Jennifer. Where did you go?'

'What do you mean? I went to art school and then I went to America and then my work took me all over the world and then I came home.'

'To Hamilton Terrace?'

'No. That's where I lived when I was a student.'

I shuddered. 'We have lost so much time, Jennifer.'

'Speak for yourself.' She turned another page.

'Where were you in America?'

'You know where.'

'You and me?'

'No. That was later.'

'You said *we*.'

'Yes. I was in Cape Cod with our son.'

'You were so lovely, Jennifer. You wore sandals made from car tyres. And a kimono with a dragon embroidered on the back.'

'Yes,' she said, 'I remember the sandals and that kimono. And you too, Saul. Your long black hair and olive skin and cheekbones and lips. We had such an appetite for each other.'

I reached for her new older hand with my new older hand.

'But tell me, Jennifer, why did you turn me down when I asked you to marry me? Is it because you knew I was attracted to men?'

'No. Not at all. I knew you fancied me too.'

'Why then?'

'You know why.'

9

When I asked Jennifer to marry me, I was looking through the bedroom door, which had somehow opened of its own accord while we were making love.

Her flatmate Claudia had just come out of the sauna to turn off the boiling kettle in the kitchen. She was naked apart from a pink towel wrapped around her head. Her stomach was flat and tanned. I was looking at her when I asked Jennifer to marry me. I wanted to keep all my options open, even as the words I was saying were supposed to close them. Jennifer wanted to keep her options open, too. There was a letter, an official-looking invitation to America, folded between the pages of her passport. She knew the worth of the art she was making for her graduation show and that it would blow her away from Britain and away from me. Had I wanted to stop her career from its immense lift-off when she was so young? Had I wanted to keep her chained to my side with my marriage proposal? Maybe, but why had I made sure she could see me looking at Claudia? I'd wanted to tell her that I had eyes, too. Jennifer was always looking at me through the lens of her camera. I often woke up with my lips pressed against her knees because she was lying at an odd angle, her camera in her hands. There were times I would pretend to sleep and then suddenly open my eyes to catch her out. Jennifer was making a career from looking. At me.

*

'Not just at you,' older Jennifer said, 'I was mostly looking at my friend, Saanvi. It was my photos of her that got me the residency in America. Why not ask me what kind of camera I was using in those days?'

'Tell me.'

'I worked with a Leica M2, the very best at the time. It belonged to my father.'

'Why are you here, with me, Jennifer?'

'Why do you think, Saul?'

'I really don't know.'

'You do know.'

'Tell me again.'

'Because you are the father of my son. Isaac died in America when he was four.'

'I know. I know he died. How did it happen?'

'No one knew he had meningitis. Not the doctor. Not me. It happened very quickly. We buried our son together.'

'Oh, Jennifer. Come closer.'

I held her hand. And I kissed it. And then I placed her hand under my shirt on my chest with my hand over hers. 'Really,' I said, 'I had no idea how to be the man you wanted me to be. I have only just started to feel things and I don't even know what year I am in.' I entwined my new older fingers through her new older fingers. We could both feel my heartbeat going berserk. We stayed like that for the whole night, her hand on my chest near my heart, my hand on top of hers, her silver hair falling over my face. It was so very comforting not to be left alone at night with the spectres.

'You took our son to America,' I was suddenly shouting. 'You more or less kidnapped my son.'

The sun was rising over the Euston Road. We could both see strips of orange sky through the blinds.

'It's like this, Jennifer Moreau' – my voice was surprisingly loud: 'I have not forgiven you.'

'I have not forgiven you either, Saul Adler.'

Our hands were still entwined. Speaking for myself, I could have died right then.

'I have no memory of Isaac. I can't see his face.'

'He will come back.'

'I don't think I could bear that.'

'You will survive.'

I looked into her eyes. For a long time. I saw that she had survived, but she was different.

'Tell me about ylang-ylang.'

'It's a flower,' she said, 'and a kind of antidepressant and an aphrodisiac. It grows in the rainforests of Indonesia and Java.'

We must have both slept for a while. It's true that my son's face came back to me. I described him to her and she said, 'Yes. Yes, that's right. Shall we carry on talking about America?'

I nodded with my new old head that was nearly sixty.

'You promise you won't walk away?'

'I promise,' she said. 'That wouldn't be fair because you can't walk away.'

10

Jennifer is twenty-eight and I am thirty-three. Our son is sick. The year is 1993. He has a few days of life left in him, but we do not yet know this. I have taken the first flight to Boston and then a ferry. A car is waiting for me in Provincetown harbour. I have been holding my sick son in a room in the clapboard house in Wellfleet, Cape Cod, for five hours. It is late afternoon and Jennifer suggests I get some fresh air in the garden. I am lying under a cherry tree in the garden of the house in Cape Cod. In the garden next door is a woman, maybe twenty-six. She is playing her cello on the wooden deck. The same piece of music over and over again. It is a pleasure to listen to her attempt to learn the language of that music. It is humming with life and hope. The woman looks up from her giant instrument, the bow in her hand, her back very straight and poised, and sees me lying under the tree. I wave, a very limp wave. I tell her I'm going to swim in the bay. The tide is in. Does she want to swim with me?

Yes, she does. She does want to swim with me. She stands up, her hand lightly resting on her cello, which looks lonely from the sudden absence of her body.

I wait for her to appear again, not believing she will come back, but she does. Her copper hair is shining in the sun, her green eyes are glittering, she seems to be phosphorescent, like a firefly or moss that can glow in the darkness of the night. I am delirious with exhaustion and I am frightened. No one seems to know what is wrong with my son. She walks through the hedge that has an arch carved into it, and when she enters our part of the garden, she stops and flinches. I turn around to where she is looking. Jennifer is standing behind me under the cherry tree. A wind is up. The blossom falls like pink rain.

'Yes,' older Jennifer said. 'I watched you both head off to the bay.'

'I was out of my mind,' I whispered from my bed in the Euston Road.

The phosphorescent, copper-haired woman took my hand and we waded into the shallow bay with its little crabs and floating weeds. She was telling me all about herself. I said nothing at all. I was pleased not to talk about my sick son. She was on vacation and renting the house next door. She was reading literature at Harvard and she played her cello in an orchestra. Her main task that summer was to learn the music I had heard her practising in the garden. In a few weeks' time she would be playing in a concert in Boston. She was open-minded and interesting and appreciated the attention and the company of the man who was listening to her. He had all the time in the world to be with her, it seemed, to swim and collect shells and frolic in the warm shallow water. The sun shone on her bright copper hair. We lay on our stomachs in the water, our shoulders touching, looking out at the sand slopes and white reeds and families unpacking picnics. It was as if she were a demonic python with her glittering eyes and long tanned legs, her soft hands deceptively strong, reaching out to me under the big American sky. She had just arrived in Wellfleet, Cape Cod, and knew nothing about my son, Isaac, who was unwell and would not survive, though I did not know that then. I liked it that she lived in another sort of reality, of books and music and the first few days of a vacation and a concert to look forward to in the future.

It was so different from my own reality, because soon, very soon, we would be performing the rituals of our son's death.

*

139

'No,' older Jennifer said, sitting by my side, 'no, she was not the python, don't make her the thing that you were. You were the snake in the reeds. You walked away when I most needed you.'

'You were anti-need,' I said coldly. 'That was your thing, you didn't need me.'

'There was no point in depending on you.' She pulled her hand away from mine. 'You were anti-dependency right from the start.'

'It's like this, Jennifer Moreau: that is why you were attracted to me in the first place.'

Jennifer flicked a strand of her silver hair over her shoulder. In the dark I could see her beauty, her poise and grace.

'It's like this, Saul Adler: I had a baby when I was twenty-four. Isaac was with me every day while I worked. We were happy. We loved each other. Many other people loved him too. He died in my arms and you were ten minutes away, but you were not there.'

Her phone was beeping. 'Don't take that call': I was steely now. 'We are just beginning. We are on to something interesting.'

I snatched the beeping phone from her hand.

'You took our son to America.' I was shouting again.

She stood up and started to walk away. The door was open and I could see her making her way through the long, eerie corridor towards the exit. Her heels clattered across the floor. 'You more or less kidnapped my son,' I shouted through the door. 'We should be together, you know we should.'

Jennifer kept on walking.

'We are attached.' I was surprised at the volume of my voice.

She turned around and suddenly ran back towards me with such force and purpose I was terrified.

'You,' she said, 'know nothing. Nothing. Nothing. Nothing about me and nothing about you.'

She was sobbing as she leaned forward and slapped my hand until her phone fell to the floor. When she stooped down to pick it up, I knew in the moment of drifting off, which I often do when things get overwhelming, that Wolfgang had paid for my private room. It was something to do with the phone.

Rainer appeared from wherever he lived in the walls of the hospital. He pulled Jennifer away from my bed and walked her out of my world. She was speaking on the phone in the eerie light of the corridor. I heard her bracelets jangling on her arm as she spoke. She sounded like she was speaking to a teenage child.

'If you've lost your bank card, you need to go to the bank with your passport and draw out some cash.'

After I had frolicked in the bay with the copper-haired woman, she told me about the music she was learning for her concert. It turned out to be a Scottish folk song. She was practising Nina Simone's version of that song to accompany the pianist on her cello. She sang it to me on the way back through the reeds. The first line was 'Black is the colour of my true love's hair.' That day, when I betrayed Jennifer under the cherry tree, I had discovered a terrible cruelty within myself. I glanced at her leaning against the wall in the corridor, her bracelets glittering on her arm.

'No, don't do that,' Jennifer said quietly into her phone. 'Ask your father to give you some money until you sort it out.'

Wolfgang was still waiting to speak to me. I knew I had to make myself available to him as he sighed behind the vase of sunflowers. His mane of silver wolfish hair would have freaked out Luna. He was standing by my bed, a camel coat draped over his shoulders, his eyelids quivering as he mouthed my name.

Soorl. Soorl. Soorl.

He was nervous and his vulnerability made me bolder.

'Yes, we have met before, Wolfgang. You were swimming in Erich Honecker's lake.'

I knew he preferred to swim on his back and that he was exhausted from inventing phenomenology, along with Husserl and Heidegger.

'Have you retired from your directorship of the university?'

'I have never been director of a university. I manage a number of hedge funds.'

Silence and sighing from Wolfgang.

His Jaguar had crashed into my head on Abbey Road and travelled with me to East Berlin, but it was already in Luna's head. That was where the regime wanted her jaguar to be. Inside her head. At night it threatened to drag her off and punish her for her thoughts. I could feel Luna's breath very close to me: she was somewhere nearby. I wanted to comfort her because I thought I knew how to, but she was not listening. She wanted to swap the Spree for the Mersey and would do anything to get there. *Bang. I love you. Rock and roll. You are my boyfriend now. If only you could dance too*, she had said, *we could try a* pas de deux, *which means 'steps for two'*. With the support of someone else helping with the lifts, she would be able to accomplish more than on her own.

I had not been listening.

Wolfgang was fumbling with his right hand in his coat pocket. He found what he was looking for. It was a handkerchief. A blue-and-white checked handkerchief folded into a neat square. He passed it to me, but I don't know why. He has a secret, I whispered to Luna, who was definitely nearby. I wiped my eyes with his handkerchief while he gathered his thoughts. They were heavy thoughts. So heavy, he lowered his silver head.

'But, Soorl.'

Where was the nurse with my morphine?

He raised his head.

'I want to talk about how you crossed the road. This is not to excuse myself or to chastise you. It is something else.'

I gave him back the handkerchief. After a while he put it away, an agonizingly slow procedure. He glanced at his shoes and then he lifted his head and looked at me.

'Yes, Wolfgang, you are going to tell me I was careless.'

I could see his eyes shining in the dark.

'No. It was a very deliberate action on your part. You were not careless at all. In fact you were very focused on getting yourself run over that day.'

I told him, coldly, that his insurance would cover the cost of the damage to his car.

'But what about damage to myself?'

He lifted his right arm to point to his left arm under the coat that was draped over his shoulders.

It was covered in a plaster cast, right up to the shoulder. He leaned forward so I could look more closely. His eyes were quivering because there was a small cut at the edge of one of his upper eyelids that had been stitched, and there were other scars, raw and recent.

I remembered Walter stretching out Wolf's arms in the lake. The way Wolf drove us home, with only one hand on the steering wheel, both of them whispering while I pretended to sleep.

He doesn't care about his own life so he doesn't care about the lives of others.

Wolfgang was standing very still on the polished floor of my private hospital room.

I could still hear Jennifer talking on her phone. *Black is the colour of my true love's hair.* She must have heard that song as I walked back to the clapboard house.

'The way you crossed the road. You nearly succeeded. You have survived because someone donated his blood to you.'

The fatal blush was beginning to welt into my body. I was blushing with the help of adrenaline and a stranger's blood. The dilating veins in my cheeks were telling Wolfgang that I was mortified. I tried to breathe. There was a coppery taste in my mouth. My mother's accident and my accident were still blurred in my mind, as was Isaac's death, which I still could not feel. I wanted to die of shame but everyone insisted on keeping me alive. I had to live. I had to live this moment now with Wolfgang. I don't think I'd had a normal life since Isaac's death, or since my meeting with Walter Müller and his family. When I crossed the road that day, I was a man in pieces.

I must have said this out loud.

'I was a man in pieces.'

'Yes,' Wolfgang said, 'I own that photograph.'

12

Three years after Isaac died and Jennifer and I had truly separated, I made the pilgrimage to see Jennifer's first solo exhibition at a gallery in Chelsea, New York. It was the opening night and I had not been invited. When Jack sent me a newspaper cutting about the show, I decided to gatecrash the private view. He offered to come with me, but I declined his company.

My excuse was that if Jennifer Moreau and I murdered each other, it was best he did not appear to be my accomplice.

Jennifer wore a long white dress. She was thirty-one and I was thirty-six. My hair was still black and her hair was now silver. She was happy that night. Jennifer stood to the right of the largest black-and-white photograph of myself, age twenty-eight. He took up the whole wall. His lips were slightly parted. His face was impassive, cold, detached. The image stopped at his narrow waist and the start of his pubic hair. A triptych on the left wall was titled *A Man in Pieces*. His armpits, nipples, fingers, penis, feet, lips, ears. Floating in space and time. From my place at the back of the gallery, I listened to Jennifer speak. She never once mentioned my name or exposed me as the subject of her visual interrogation. The man in pieces had dead eyes. The curator made a speech too. Something about the blurring of the triptych, the head shot in profile, the long exposure and the shutter speed and placing a subject next to the edge of the page so the eye is drawn to it. Her words were a blur to me as well. Something about loneliness, love, youth, beauty. When Jennifer was a student working with oil paint she was always searching for a studio with enough light. After she took up her camera she practically lived in the dark room. It was there she discovered that developing a photograph was similar to being a painter.

There is a spectre inside every photograph.

Various fashionably dressed women and men gathered around her. A tall man lingered nearby. He was dressed entirely in black. Every now and again he whispered in her ear or brought her a glass of champagne. I noticed that he was carrying her bag. When she was steered to the far end of the gallery and he stood stranded at the other end, he lifted up his glass to acknowledge her wave. I was glad not to be him.

I watched the crowd looking at the photographs, while I, the trespasser, uninvited, also gazed at my younger self sleeping in that flat on Hamilton Terrace, as represented by Jennifer, who had forbidden me to describe her.

I was very calm. I was waiting to be recognized. But no one spoke to me. No one said, 'Is that you?'

At one point I took three glasses of champagne from a silver tray and drank all of them in five seconds. No one noticed I was there. After a while I walked away from the crowd and took refuge in the men's bathroom. While I was sitting on the toilet with my jeans around my knees, a biro fell out of my pocket. I picked it up and wrote on the toilet wall in tiny letters. When I gazed at the words I realized I was drunk.

a man in pieces wox hare

I was staggering when I made my way back into the exhibition. No one so much as glanced at the drunk spectre haunting it. I had already knocked back two pints of Guinness in an Irish pub near the gallery before I arrived. To be so insignificant and yet to be the subject of

Jennifer's show was hard to take. At the same time, I did not understand what kind of significance I was after. I did not want to be the man carrying her bag. If I was merely an artist's model, why would I expect to be acknowledged, even to be praised or publicly thanked? Yet we had been lovers. We were intimately and tragically connected to each other. Why was I here alone? That is what Jack had asked me. 'Why would you go alone?' He had offered his support and I had rejected it. At least he could not see me now, uninvited, envious and enraged. I was all over the walls but my name was not on the guest list.

And then she saw me. Everything became slow and weird. I could feel her heartbeat and I knew she could feel mine. In her white dress she walked towards me. The crowds parted as she made her way to where I was standing. She was mortal and I was mortal and Isaac was mortal (oh God) but her art was immortal and filled every wall in the room. I knew that she considered art itself to be bigger than myself and bigger than herself, but I was not that interested in art. Now she was facing me, everything went quiet and queasy and still. I could hear her inhaling and exhaling and I saw her (again) standing on the doorstep having just pushed me out of her flat, her camera in her hands. *So long, Saul. You'll always be my muse.*

All my body was trembling.

'Hello, Saul. What are you doing here?'

'I'm already here, Jennifer.' I pointed to the photographs on the wall.

I looked up and saw another image. It was the photograph of myself crossing Abbey Road when I was twenty-eight.

'That's Luna's photo.'

'Well, you might have given a copy to Luna but I took the photograph.' She laughed in my face. 'In fact,' she said, 'I carried a ladder for a mile to Abbey Road to take it.'

The female curator who had made the speech suddenly appeared at her side.

She was Jennifer's protector, her guard dog. I suppose there was a lot of money at stake in the photographs.

She placed her hand on Jennifer's arm and invited me to look again at the walls. This time I noticed there were other photographs.

So many of them.

Jennifer standing in profile, naked and pregnant in the doorway of the clapboard house; Isaac sitting in the sand of the bay at Wellfleet, burying his small foot in the sand; Isaac sleeping in the shadow of his mother taking the photograph, as if he had returned to her womb; the new but ancient fists of our son raised to his ears in a rage; the cherry tree in the garden with its abundant blossom, and, underneath it, a toy wooden train; a cello standing abandoned on a sundeck; a tiny shoe decorated with seashells from Wellfleet Bay, and when I looked more closely, I saw the shells made the first letter of Isaac's name, *I*, and then the same *I* written with stones on the sand of the beach. The tide had come in and the *I* was slipping into the sea; another *I* drawn with a stick on the sand slopes of Marconi Beach, a single vowel that was being pecked at by a gull, as if it sensed a worm lurked under the sand on which the *I* was written.

Jennifer Moreau gestured to the walls.

'It's not about you. It's about me.'

13

Wolfgang seemed agitated and excited. His damaged eyelid was quivering. He wore a cologne that smelled of leather – perhaps the marbled doeskin leather seats of his now-extinct Jaguar.

'I own that photograph,' he whispered again, in his posh, strained voice.

'It is one of my most loved acquisitions.'

'She never asked me.' I could feel some sort of physical pain returning to the whole of my body. 'She rejected me all the time but she wanted to possess me.'

He waited patiently while the Irish nurse administered my morphine.

'I saw you before I saw you on Abbey Road.' Wolfgang touched his throat with the hand that was not in plaster. 'I own a Jennifer Moreau.'

I sipped the morphine gratefully in my new private room while the nurse pretended to stare at the wall. I knew she was watching me all the same, like the woman who gave a cauliflower to Walter on the day I arrived in the GDR. She too had been staring elsewhere while watching me intensely.

'I hear I'm going home in a week?'

She nodded absently.

Wolfgang had become increasingly nervous. He paced around the room in his shiny banker's shoes, sighing and grinding his teeth.

'Wolf, can I ask you a question?'

'Yes, Soorl.'

'Have you and I ever planted tomatoes together?'

He shook his head. 'I'm not the gardening type.'

'I don't think he is the gardening type either.'

'Who is "he"?'

'I don't know. He's staying away. Keeping his distance.'

The physical pain had disappeared with the morphine. I was crying anyway.

Wolfgang stepped forward with another question.

'Do you have family?'

'Yes. A brother.'

He seemed agitated to hear this news. It occurred to me that he thought I might be dying. I wiped my eyes with the sheet. Wolfgang offered me his handkerchief again, but I refused to take it. After a while, I explained that my brother was my next of kin.

'He's a thug,' I said. 'He will come after your houses and your shares and all your acquisitions.'

I did not tell him that my father had raised my brother and myself in the spirit of socialism. We were to be highly principled and never exploit anyone to get rich.

Wolfgang raised his head and stared at the ceiling.

'I suppose,' he said, 'that when you crossed the road I saw a moment of despair.'

'I suppose you did.'

We both knew he had been speaking on his phone when he ran me over. I think he was waiting for me to point this out. He stood in silence, like a wounded silver beast, watching me weep, fearful my family would sue him. He was now trying to barter my despair for my silence. When I finally accepted his handkerchief, I told him it was not in my nature to point the finger. It was the better side of my carelessness. He seemed relieved and told me to keep the handkerchief. No. I didn't want it. I told him to hang on to his possessions and acquisitions. For a start, I had his Jaguar inside my head. His wing mirror, from which he had glimpsed the man in pieces crossing the road, had shattered. A thousand and one slivers of glass were floating inside my head.

I had gazed at my reflection in his wing mirror and my reflection had fallen into me. It was not just my spleen that preoccupied Rainer. Apparently, I was to be nourished later in the day via some tubes that would be placed in my nostrils. Should I eat one of the sunflowers? It was a question I wanted to ask my friend Jack. He was always hungry, after all, especially after a day spent in the garden. Sometimes I feared that Rainer, as well as the night nurse, did not expect to see me in the morning. Where did they think I would be? Offering my kisses like coins to Jack in return for his labour?

14

I looked into the mirror for the first time since my accident. *Fuck off I hate you*, I said to the middle-aged man staring back at me. His hair had been shaved. He was a skull. His eyes a shock of blue in his pale face. He had high cheekbones. A cut on the cheek and on the lip. His eyebrows were silver. Where have you gone, Saul? All that beauty blown to bits. Who were you? What languages do you speak? Are you a son and a brother and a father? Are you an acquisition? How do you get along with your female colleagues? What is the point of them, in your view? What is the point of yourself, in their view? Are you there to do something for them? Or are they there to do something for you? Are they a foil for your ambitions or are you a foil for theirs? In what ways do you thwart, oppose, derail or support each other? Which way do you vote? Are you a good historian? Did you ever play football? Cricket? Ping-pong? Are you curious about other people? Or do you walk on the outer edges of life, indifferent, remote, tormented by the affection human beings seem to feel for each other? Are other men envious of you? Are you loving? Have you ever been loved? *Yes, I have been loved and I am loving*, I said to the man in the mirror, *I am all those things I am I am and I need to know what happened to Walter Müller.*

'You know what happened to Walter Müller.'

Jennifer was reading a book at my side. Her hair had turned blue-black in the light. She was floating like cells under a microscope as she pressed the book against the curve of her breasts. 'You saw him on your thirtieth birthday.'

15

I am being shaved by a Turkish barber in West Berlin. It is January 1990 and snow is falling. The Wall that once divided the country in two is now being sold in pieces as souvenirs to tourists. The barber throws a towel over my shoulders, tilts my head back, moves a brush of foam over my cheeks and jaw and under my chin. My ears fill with foam, too. He picks up a razor, unscrews the blade and puts in another one, silver and sharp. He places his hand on my head and moves in with the blade, starting somewhere near my ear, moving down my cheeks, tipping my head, steering his blade under my chin, wiping the foam on his wrist. His finger holds my nostrils as he moves to my upper lip. I open my mouth. Walter has not answered my phone calls or letters, nor has his mother, nor his colleagues at the university, so it is a surprise that he has finally made contact with me. The radio is on. The barber grabs my head and pushes it down into a basin. He washes my hair with shampoo and rinses it with the tap shower, pulls my head up, places a towel over it. He massages my forehead. Trims my eyebrows with the help of a comb and scissors. Rubs cream into his palms and moisturizes my face. This is how I prepared for my lunch date with Walter Müller. Even after my shave I still had two hours to spare.

To pass time I walked to the tall building in Mitte to look once again at the copper relief of the astronaut called *Man Overcomes Space and*

Time. He was young, noble and determined. If he set his mind to it he could orbit the earth and trick gravity, yet at the same time he was frozen, fixed in the past. Time was passing very slowly. Time was crawling. The cold air grazed my newly shaved face. I talked to an elderly man eating the soup he had purchased from a wagon parked on the pavement. He told me that he had lived most of his life in the East. Now it was every man for himself. No one cared that his family had lost their jobs. He had no money to travel and could not afford to shop in the well-stocked supermarkets of the West. If he had his way he would build the Wall again, except twelve metres higher. I glanced at my watch. Time had at last staggered forward. I hailed a cab to 58 Kurfürstenstraße, where I had arranged to meet Walter at Café Einstein, an old Viennese coffee house and restaurant, leaving my companion to finish his meat-and-pickled-vegetable soup in the snow.

When Walter eventually walked through the doors of Café Einstein, twenty minutes late, he was wearing the grey overcoat he'd worn to meet me at the station two years previously. His hair was cropped, he was thinner, he was smiling, he was in a hurry. He looked apologetic as he fumbled with his wet gloves. I stood up and he kissed my lips, lightly, airily, as if it were a summer day and snow was not falling. He seemed distracted and refused to sit down.

'You still have your hair,' he said in English.

He knew I had booked this table three weeks in advance of our meeting. He was agitated and kept glancing at his watch.

'Please sit down, Walter. Can I buy you a coffee? A beer? Lunch?'

'No, nothing at all. I have to go soon.'

I was hurt and disappointed. When the waiter passed our table, I ordered two espressos. Walter finally sat down.

I asked him about life now that the border was open.

'I miss the parties,' Walter said. 'We had a lot of parties in the East. Mostly, life is better.'

He dropped a sugar lump into his coffee and stirred it with the tiny silver teaspoon for a long time. The spoon scratched against the porcelain as he stirred, on and on. The astronaut on the statue in Mitte would have made it from Jupiter to Mars by the time Walter eventually lifted the cup to his lips.

He said he had a sense that he was panicking every day. It was hard to make a living as a translator, to pay the new rent and new bills. He put on his spectacles and finally looked more directly into my eyes. The coffee seemed to have perked him up. My subject was communist Eastern Europe but I could not speak the languages. He could speak all the Eastern European languages. He was distinguished and clever but he didn't think so. I waved to the waiter and ordered Walter another coffee. He told me he liked the sugar lumps in the silver bowl, white and pale gold. I asked him to say that in Polish and Czech.

'Say what?'

'The sugar lumps, white and pale gold.'

He found the words as snow fell on the roofs of the taxis parked outside. He told me he didn't yet know his way around Berlin and had to ask for directions. He looked sadder without his long mousy hair.

I invited him to London to speak to my students about growing up in the GDR.

Walter seemed neither interested nor uninterested. I wondered if he respected me as a historian, or even as a friend. He glanced at the tray a waiter was carrying above his shoulder to a table nearby. It was loaded with schnitzel and potato salad and two glasses of champagne the colour of spring daffodils.

'I can order that for us,' I said. 'Please have lunch with me.' I reached out for his hand. He was always good at touching back, and he did. This small moment of intimacy made me braver.

'Tell me what happened, Walter, after we said goodbye in Alexanderplatz.' I had been tormented for two years by the vision of that van pulling up on the pavement beside him. When he had not responded to my efforts to get in touch with him, I concluded that he must have been pushed into the van by unsmiling grey men. They would have intimidated him with guns and rubber truncheons. He would have been interrogated because I gave Rainer, who was an informer, a substantial sum of money to help him escape. Yet I had not asked Walter if he wanted to leave.

'The border has opened since we said goodbye,' he said. 'But on that afternoon, I believe I ate a very tasty sausage.'

He was not laughing. Walter used to be good at laughing. Such a sexy laugh. When our knees touched under the table, he glanced again at his watch.

'I don't think you ate a sausage that afternoon,' I said. 'You told me you were scheduled to teach English to men and women who had good careers but who were going to build socialism elsewhere, including Ethiopia.'

'Correct. It was not a sausage. It was a dumpling.'

I asked him why it had taken him so long to get in touch with me.

'We had to move to another apartment,' he said, as if that explained everything.

A woman walked into Café Einstein wheeling a pram, holding the hand of a girl, maybe three years old. She was told to leave the pram outside, at which point Walter stood up and walked over to help her. He scooped up the baby that was asleep in the pram, and then pointed to me. The woman and her daughter made their way to my table. She was in her thirties and had neat, short blond hair, as did her daughter. Their hair was cut in exactly the same style, short at the back and sides, with a long fringe. Snow was melting on their coats. People were in their way. Chairs had to be moved, tables rearranged, conversations interrupted as she picked up her daughter and swung her over the heads of customers tucking into plates of pork. Her small brown eyes were bright. She had a mole above her lip.

'Hallo,' she said, 'my name is Helga. I am Walter's wife. And this is our daughter, Hannah.'

I had reserved a table for two. There were now four of us, because Walter was making his way through the crowded restaurant with a baby draped over his shoulder. With the waiter's help we had to find a bigger table. Walter handed their new child to Helga and went off to hang up their coats. They were a family. His wife was wearing a polo-neck jumper, jeans and trainers. The women dining in Einstein wore cashmere cardigans and leather boots.

'This is our son, Karl Thomas,' she said, gesturing to Hannah to sit on the chair next to her.

'I'm Saul,' I said to Walter's daughter. 'How old is the baby?'

Hannah told me in German that he was seven months.

When Walter returned I ordered three beers and a hot chocolate for the child. Karl Thomas sucked his fingers as Helga passed him back to Walter. Hannah took off her gloves. Walter was preoccupied with the top three buttons on the baby's snowsuit. Helga searched in her bag, looking for a toy for Hannah. It was all quite boring. They were discussing feeding Karl Thomas. Walter was now using a napkin to clean the teat on a bottle of milk. His hands were gentle as he coaxed the teat into the lips of his son. Hannah threw the cutlery on to the floor. Helga calmly told her to pick it up. Her daughter refused. It was dull to be there with them all. Helga shouted at her and Hannah started to cry. Helga found a box of crayons and paper in her bag and suggested her daughter sit on her lap. Hannah shook her head and crawled under the table. All conversation had stopped. It was as if the family were an organism, each part depending on the other part to survive the next two minutes. They did not seem bored or happy or unhappy. Helga had now persuaded her daughter to come out from under the table. This small triumph seemed to please them all.

I turned to Walter. 'How is your sister?'

It was the second question I had been most nervous of asking my East German lover. I still did not know if Luna had told her brother about our night together in the dacha.

Walter looked into Karl Thomas's eyes as he fed him. He was smiling as the baby gulped down the milk. It was Helga who answered my question.

'We don't know whether Luna is alive or dead.'

She lifted Hannah on to her lap and started to draw a cat with a green crayon.

'What happened to Luna?'

'She escaped one month before they opened the border.'

Their eyes were on me. Six pairs of eyes. My breath was bitter from too much coffee.

'But hasn't she contacted you?'

'We haven't heard from her.'

Helga was now drawing whiskers on the cat. Hannah, who had an orange crayon in her hand, added a long curved tail. The beers and hot chocolate had arrived.

'Walter, I need to speak to you alone.'

'Okay,' he said, 'but I was looking forward to my beer.'

He passed the baby to Helga, which meant Hannah had to get off her lap. When she started to wail, I pushed him away from his wife and his beer and his children.

We sat on the steps of Café Einstein in the snow. He offered me a cigarette but I had something to say to him before I could smoke. I lit his cigarette with my Zippo.

'I am very sorry, Walter, for being so foolish with Rainer.'

'Yes, it was careless,' Walter replied.

My newly shaved face was burning up. It was like fire in the snow.

'I have done things that I regret too,' he said.

'What sort of things?'

He stared at the glowing tip of his new brand of cigarette and did not reply.

'Walter, we must find Luna. Do you think she made it to the West?'

'For now, we have to live without knowing.'

'That must be very hard.'

'Yes. Hardest for my mother.'

He glanced at my blushing face.

'She would have left anyway. Without your intervention. Rainer already knew she wanted to leave.'

We smoked and stared at the snow.

'She will be in Liverpool,' I declaimed with great certainty. 'I believe she is there because the wish in her was so fierce.'

Walter's spectacles were now covered in snow crystals.

'There is one very good reason for her to be in touch,' he said.

'What is that?'

'Karl Thomas.'

He told me that Karl Thomas was Luna's son. When he was four months old she left him with their mother for the day and she never returned.

Luna is short for lunatic, I thought, but did not say that out loud. What sort of woman betrays her son like that? He would miss her every day, see her everywhere, wonder what he did wrong to make his mother disappear, ask himself if it was his fault, did she not like him enough to stay around? I was furious with Luna so I asked about Rainer.

'No one knows what happened to Rainer, either. He was the person with knowledge and contacts for those who wished to leave the republic. But that October he disappeared alongside Luna.'

I could feel the blush spreading over my chest and up my neck.

Walter noticed and he laughed.

'I never told you about my wife and daughter.' He squeezed his eyes against the falling snow.

'That's all right with me. You had to make your own arrangements.'

This time I accepted a cigarette.

'Walter, I am a father too. I have a son.'

He looked startled, truly amazed. He lifted his right hand, combed it through his hair and then stamped the snow off his boots.

'What's his name?'

'Isaac.'

'And where is he now?'

'In America with his mother.'

'Why didn't you tell me this first? Before anything else?'

'I am separated from his mother. She left with our son.'

'I'm sorry.' He thumped his hand on my thigh.

I suddenly realized I was ravenous. I had not eaten breakfast or lunch. I felt light-headed and hot and cold in the snow.

'Walter, you are free to travel now. Maybe in August you can join me in the cottage I have bought in Suffolk. Why not make your honey farm in my garden? I am lonely and you are lonely.'

Walter laughed again. It was as if he had become the old Walter in the old Germany. This encouraged me to say more about the kind of life we might live together, which I did, in some detail.

He lightly draped his arm around my shoulders.

'Where are my children when I stay with you in this Suffolk place in August?'

'They are with Helga.'

'Helga is an engineer. She earns the money for our family.'

'I will pay for your travel,' I insisted.

'Will Isaac be with you in this house in Suffolk?'

I explained that he lived with Jennifer in America and that I would see him in the summer holidays.

'But August is the summer holidays. You would be better off making a honey farm with your son.'

He jumped up from the steps with something of his old energy. He seemed anxious to return to his beer. I followed him. Helga had finished her beer and was halfway through mine. Hannah was now playing with six red buttons threaded with string. Karl Thomas was sleeping on Helga's lap. Someone thumped my shoulder. It was the waiter bringing me the bill. As the family put on their coats and hats and gloves, Helga prodded my arm.

'If you want, you can give us some money to help with Karl Thomas.'

She glanced at my blue linen shirt and when I did not reply she did this strange thing with her arms. She put both hands behind her back, palms together like a prayer, her fingers pointing towards the chandelier.

'It's my new yoga position,' she said.

Walter looked embarrassed as he zipped up Hannah's coat. It was hard to believe he was the man who had kissed me in the forest as we crouched under the branches of a tree, or the man who had got me drunk on schnapps and then cooked supper, naked, laughing and flirtatious.

'Hey, Saul, this is for you.' He pressed a brown envelope into my hand. 'I found it in my mother's apartment.'

It was addressed to me in Jennifer's handwriting and still had the English stamps lined up on the top-right corner. They left together, Helga empty-handed, whatever the position of her hands. In a way it was a relief to be alone again.

I sat down at the table with its three empty chairs and opened the envelope. Inside it was the photograph I had given Luna of myself in a white suit crossing Abbey Road in 1988. It had been savagely ripped into two pieces. I understood that it was Luna's revenge for smashing her precious *Abbey Road* album under my boots. In a way it was fair enough but it was a shock to see myself in pieces. My cheeks were still tender from the Turkish barber's sharp blade.

As I put the pieces of the photograph back in the envelope, I realized something else was inside it. One sheet of thin paper folded in half. The paper was covered with typewritten words, some of them crossed out. At first glance it seemed to be an interview between Walter and someone else. The subject of the conversation was the letter I had written to him in East Germany, declaring my love for him.

Please, Herr Müller, we want to know more about your English friend, Saul Adler. Will you help us?

Yes.

What is the meaning of this line here? In this letter he has written to you.

The words mean to put the palm of his hand or his fingertips on the stomach of his correspondent to better understand how he is feeling.

And what is the feeling?

Friendship.

Why would a man place his hand on the stomach of another man to better understand a feeling?

You will have to interrogate the hand.

Did you have sexual relations with your English friend Saul Adler?

If you are asking me if I have plans to leave the East and live elsewhere, I have no plans to leave.

What is the meaning of this sentence here referring to the Baltic Sea in winter?

The words mean the correspondent wishes to see the Baltic Sea in winter.

And is the Baltic Sea a code for something else in this context?

You will have to interrogate the Baltic Sea.

No, we will interrogate your sister instead. We believe she is pregnant with Herr Adler's child. Is this your understanding, too?

You will have to interrogate his penis.

I sat alone with the white linen tablecloths and silver cutlery, watching the Berlin snow fall outside the window. More than anything, I wanted to leave earth and join the astronaut on his mission to walk across the surface of the moon.

Older Jennifer was at my side as she had promised she would be.
    'So what did you do next?'
    'I left Café Einstein and bought a kebab.'

That night a warm wind lifted the blossom off the cherry tree in Massachusetts and blew it into Abbey Road, London.

I heard Luna singing 'Penny Lane' in the pink rain.

A shabby plain woman sat on the chair beside my bed in my new private hospital room. She was eating a cherry-flavoured yogurt from a plastic pot.

'Hello, Helga,' I said. 'Did you enjoy your yoga class in Berlin?'

'I'm not Helga, I'm Tessa,' she replied. 'Your sister-in-law. Matt's wife.'

'No, you are Walter's fake wife.'

'No. I'm your brother's real wife.'

'Oh, it's all coming back to me.' I waved my hands as if somehow this gesture would magic her out of my world, but she didn't budge.

'I had to travel here from Birmingham New Street, where I've been teaching today.'

'I'm pleased you can travel freely now, Helga.'

'I'm Tessa. And the trains are not free. I teach children with special needs.'

'That will be all of us, with special needs,' I said.

'In a way it is, yes.'

She unzipped an ugly grey rucksack and took out an orange.

'Is it from Cuba?'

'Is what from Cuba?'

'Your orange.'

'I think it's from Valencia.' She pointed to a little sticker on the peel of the orange.

'Did you have to queue for a long time to buy it?'

'No. About two people in front of me.'

'You must have bought it from the Intershop,' I said, smiling. 'I suppose you used the West German marks I gave Walter.'

'I bought it from Tesco.'

'What a treat.'

'I eat oranges all the time.' She started to peel the orange. Her nails were bitten down and it took some time for her to get a grip on the peel.

'Oh, I forgot,' I said. 'The Wall is down. The border is open.'

She was wearing flesh-coloured tights and flat brown shoes made from faux leather. Her legs were crossed. The scuffed shoes, which resembled ballet shoes, were slipping off her feet.

'It must be hard,' I said kindly, 'to blend in with the more prosperous West Germans.'

'You're upsetting your brother and father,' she said.

'Yes, I've been upsetting them for ever.'

'They've been told to stay away by the hospital staff, as if they're vermin.'

'Is that why you're here to bother me, Tessa?'

'Well, at least you've got my name right.' She pushed a segment of orange into her mouth. Juice dripped down her chin. Two of her back teeth were missing.

'Look,' I said from my place propped up with pillows, 'I don't want to see you either. Please remove your yogurt pot from my table. Go away. Leave me to my sepsis and morphine and sunflowers.'

She leaned forward so her face was close to my own.

'You little shit. Do you know what your brother has been doing for you? He's been sorting out your sick pay at the university. He's been talking to your union people every day and he's knackered enough already. Your bosses point out that you're expensive to employ because of your age and you're not in a fit state to work.'

I wondered where Rainer had got to. He would see Tessa off for me. Another doctor had been doing the rounds since I'd become stronger. Or perhaps since I'd become weaker. I hadn't seen Rainer for a while.

'I have a PhD on the psychology of male tyrants,' I said, glancing at her through the golden petals of the sunflowers, 'starting with Stalin's father, Besarion Ivanes dze Jughashvili, also known as Beso. He was a shoemaker of some renown. Georgian footwear was his speciality, but, alas for him, the European style of shoe was becoming more fashionable at the time.'

Tessa took off her spectacles and slipped them into her rucksack.

'Your brother is paying your bills.'

'I still don't want to see him.'

Tessa stood up. She looked tired and furious.

'Do you have a message for Matthew?'

I touched my head and shut my eyes.

'Right,' she said. 'I'll tell him you said thank you.'

The sound of her worn-out shoes shuffling across the floor stayed with me for a long time. I had to get to another world. To Walter. To Luna, who tried to dance away her panic. To the phosphorescent woman and her cello. To the astronaut driving his Lunar Roving Vehicle across the surface of the moon.

When I opened my eyes in the dawn of the Euston Road, the first thing I saw was the plastic cherry yogurt that Tessa had left on my table. It was past its sell-by date and on special offer. Underneath the pot was a slip of paper terminating my employment at the university.

Rainer stood beside by bed.

'Welcome back to Britain. Or are you still swimming in Erich Honecker's lake?'

'I'm definitely in Britain,' I replied, though I could not feel my lips moving. 'Is it true that I can go home next week, Rainer?'

'Who told you that?'

'The night-shift nurse.'

I leaned forward and plucked a petal from one of the sunflowers, rolling it between my fingers until it became yellow mush in my hands. Rainer looked startled but he did not contradict me. As he pressed his stethoscope against my heart, he began to fade and blur into East German Rainer.

'Yes,' he said, 'it's true that we have many enemies, such as the night-shift nurse, trying to perpetrate sabotage wherever they can.' He definitely didn't sound like himself, but as I hardly knew him, how would I know that? While he listened to my heart murmur and mope, I understood his ears were the listening device hidden inside and outside his head.

18

Jennifer asked if there was anything I wished for while I lay in my bed waiting for something to happen. I could hear the sound of water between us, still and sad, and I heard my breath and the click of one of my toes.

'I'd like a bacon roll. And a bath. And to iron my shirts.'

She looked surprised. 'I thought you were going to wish big things for the world.'

'I want to walk again and meet my nephews and maybe see Jack. But Rainer says I'm going home in a week.'

When she did not reply I wondered if she was going to take out her sketchbook and tell me to visit Jack and my nephews and have a bath and iron my shirts so she could draw my visions with her pencil.

I felt her fingers somewhere on my face.

'The air is very dry in here,' she said, dabbing some sort of cream on my lips.

It was true they were blistered and sore.

'Yes,' she whispered, 'smudge them together. Like this.'

We were both looking into each other's eyes as she leaned over me.

I would have preferred to iron my shirts in all the time zones I was living in than return to Jennifer and me swimming in that pond in Cape Cod after we had buried Isaac.

'I know nothing about you, Jennifer. Nothing about your life after us.'

'That's true.'

I waited for her to speak her life to me. I waited for a long time.

'Well, ask me some questions, then,' she finally said.

I suppose I wanted to know who it was she said 'darling' and 'sweetheart' to on her phone, where she was living, how she was living. Yet I did not want to know, as well as wanting to. I could not break into her thoughts and feelings. Or my own. I could not break in.

'Jennifer, am I still forbidden to describe your body?'

'What else about me interests you?'

Her fingers had moved from my lips to somewhere under my right cheekbone. I shut my eyes. Her fingertips were gentle as she soothed the cream into my skin. But Jennifer had never been gentle. Not with me.

'It's like this, Saul Adler.'

'It's like what, Jennifer Moreau?'

'It's not as if it's my life's work to help you see me. I've got other things to do.'

'Your favourite colour is yellow,' I said with tremendous certainty.

I could hear her speaking in French to someone who was by her side. I had forgotten her father was French and that she spoke the language fluently. The person she was speaking to was not French, his accent was English. He sounded a bit like Jack. I wondered if they were speaking in French because they did not want me to understand what they were saying. But I did understand. Jennifer was explaining how she preferred travelling by train than on aeroplanes. It was easier to transport her cameras and other equipment. The person by her side asked her another question. 'Yes,' she said, 'I miss my daughters. Especially when I make pancakes in winter.'

I raised my head from the pillows. 'You have daughters, Jennifer?'

'Yes. They are both at university.'

My eyes were open and hers were closed, her eyelashes mascaraed blue.

'You know, Saul, you might be a good father.' Suddenly we were kissing. Deep kissing. In that kiss I tried to beam all my love into her.

171

'You are blooming,' I said to her. 'Your hair and eyes are shining and your breasts have become heavier.' When I placed my hand on Jennifer's stomach, she pushed it away.

'I will be a good father,' I whispered in her cold ear.

'Yes. But you would be a terrible husband.'

'We don't have to get married.'

'You're already a terrible boyfriend.'

When I told her I wanted to be with her when the baby was born, she suddenly raised her hand.

'I grew up without a father,' she said. 'What's it like to have one around?'

'Bad,' I replied.

I must have spoken that word out loud, 'bad', because I heard older Jennifer whisper in French to whoever else was by her side, 'He is still with us, but was he ever with us?'

I was very much with her after we buried Isaac, when we took off our swimming gear away from the crowds on the shores of that pond in Cape Cod. Both of us naked, frail, treading water at different ends of the longest pond. And then we made our way towards each other, which is when we saw the turtle flick between our legs. At last we touched, head to head, our arms around each other, toes sinking in the sand, sun blasting down on our shoulders. I gazed across the water to the shore. Someone was waving at Jennifer as he stood under a big New England tree. He was tall and he was holding a towel in his hands. She started to swim back to him, at first slowly, as if every movement of her arms and legs pained her, and then she picked up speed, kicking the water into a froth as she swam towards where he was waiting for her with the towel held out in his hands. We both knew the turtle that could snap at her legs was also swimming for its life somewhere nearby.

19

Matt returned alone, without his wife, who had come on her secret mission to torment me with reality. He brought no gifts. He had come straight from work so it must have been around seven at night. He was wearing a blue boiler suit. I knew he had been sure to arrive at a time when he knew Rainer's shift had ended. He had come to find me and harm me. The tips of his boots were made from lead. He carried a bag of tools. He smelled of sweat and bricks. His forehead was pink. Maybe burned from the sun, because I had begun to understand that it was summer. His big fingers were smeared with sooty dust.

I made a sign with my hands to ward him off.

He moved two steps backwards.

'I'm not going to hurt you.' He lifted his big hands and placed them over his pink face. Then he moved to a nearby sink and washed his hands with a few drops from the antibacterial soap dispenser.

'Speak to me from the sink. Don't come any closer. Stand there.'

He nodded.

'Put your big fists in the pockets of your boiler suit.'

He placed his hands, still wet from the water, in his pockets.

'Dad died last night, Saul.'

I started to drift off but only for three seconds. I opened my eyes and Matt was still standing where I had told him to stand, by the sink. His bag of tools was by his feet.

'The neighbour who brings him the newspaper found him this morning.'

He closed his brutal blue eyes.

We were both silent for about forty years.

'The grandchildren are upset,' he said.

'What grandchildren?'

'My sons.'

He glanced at his watch. His family were waiting for him to come home.

'Did they like their grandfather?'

'Oh yes.'

We were silent for another fifteen years.

'He made all the furniture in their room. The bunk beds. He made Isaac a wooden train.'

A few more decades passed between us. I was somewhere in a university town with spires and old stone buildings. I was lying in a punt on the River Cam, reading a book. It was a life I never thought I deserved. Was I allowed to want it? I was eating supper at a long wooden table in my college, wearing my black undergraduate gown. The students before me had gone on to become eminent philosophers, composers, physicists, priests, bishops, industrialists, deans, biochemists, political theorists, cricketers. What was I aiming for? What did I want? What did I deserve? I was in a tutorial in a study overlooking a square of green grass, talking about the book I had not read. My tutor stared out of the window. I was neither stupid nor brilliant, but my physical beauty gave me some gravitas. My friend Anthony's father had come to visit him. He was a banker and a Tory. My father was a builder and a communist. We got on all right. I had come from another world, but I did not want to find my way home. Anthony's father wanted to know where I went to school. And where my brother went to school. And where my father went to school. 'We were all educated at Eton,' I told him solemnly, while Anthony, who kept his signet ring in a box of cocaine under his bed, guffawed into his soft, white hands. I was asked to choose a bottle of wine from the menu. They both knew that I knew nothing about wine because it was likely my family drank beer. We ate a plate of guts in a posh restaurant and talked about the weather and traffic. The last time I had returned home to Bethnal Green we talked about the Toxteth riots in Liverpool.

'Doves,' Matt said. 'I will let off some doves for Dad.'

'He preferred his hawk.'

'Doves,' he said again.

'A dove is a small pigeon which can be disembowelled by a hawk.'

It was the sort of thing I used to say to Anthony, but it was lost on Matt.

A few months passed between us.

When I opened my eyes, Matt was still by my bed.

I pointed to the box of fudge my father had left on the table.

Matt opened the box. He waved a square past my lips.

'No,' I said. 'It will send me mad.'

'You're already mad. Can't see that a bit of fudge will make any difference.'

I closed my eyes and tried to touch my black hair. I couldn't find it so I touched my right earlobe instead.

A day passed between us. Our father had died sometime in that day. Matt was still there but he was putting on his jacket.

'Saul. I am very sorry for everything.'

My brother was trying to say something, as usual.

'I didn't take our mother passing very well either. I was a freak.'

'That's an insult to freaks,' I hissed, like the freakish swans on the Spree. 'You mean you were not stable.'

'That's it.'

'I thought I was the mad one.'

'You were the clever, good-looking one,' he replied. 'I was the crazy, ugly, stupid one.'

'That sounds about right.'

Something was wrong. I gazed at my brother's wet blue eyes. Now that I had spoken those words out loud, it was hard to put them back in again, quietly, sneakily, as if nothing had happened. He was the crazy, ugly, stupid one. *That sounds about right.* The shiny floor. My brother's dusty boots.

'Nothing is right,' I said to Matt in my head. 'Our brotherhood is not right.'

'You're saying something.' Matt took a step closer. He listened while I spoke to him. 'No, you're singing,' he said. 'You're singing "Penny Lane".' I heard a voice come out of my body, a tiny, cracked voice. Everything was loud, except for my voice. The loud clock ticking on the wall of the hospital on the Euston Road. The clock ticking in the dacha in the GDR. Luna standing on the chair in the dacha with her arms stretched out, trying to tell me she was hopeless. The saddest clock ticking in the clapboard house in Cape Cod. The watch on my dead father's wrist still ticking. I sang to my brother's wet blue eyes.

After a while he walked back to the basin.

'Is there something you want me to say for you at the funeral?'

'I'll say it for myself. I'm home in a week.'

'Who told you that?'

'The night nurse. Rainer confirmed it.'

Matt zipped up his jacket. It seemed to take him a long time and required all his attention. The zip was stuck for about ten years. Some of the grooves were missing.

'And you,' I asked, 'what will you say?'

'A few words.'

'Like what?'

The tube of light on the ceiling lit up his big sad face. He looked like a giant bald angel.

'I will give a bit of history,' he said. ' "Dad, you raised your sons alone. You grew up in East London . . ." '

' "In circumstances that were somewhat reduced," ' I offered. ' "In fact, you grew up so poor, you sold your dog at the market." '

Matt cracked a smile.

'It's true,' I said. 'There was a market in the East End where you could sell your pets if you were that broke.'

I continued from my bed.

' "Dad, after the war you carved the flesh off a dead horse and gave the meat to the poor." '

'He never did that.'

Matt's zip was still stuck. He tugged at it while he spoke.

' "Dad, you worked every hour. The house was warm in winter. We never wanted for anything. Except our mother. You read Karl Marx when you were fourteen." '

Matt paused. 'Can you help me out here? I've never read *The Communist Manifesto*. What did he see in it?'

He plucked a pen from his pocket. A small biro the size of his little finger with the name of a building society written across its side.

I cleared my throat. The sunflowers were wilting in their vase.

'Marx was just twenty-nine when he wrote *The Communist Manifesto* with Engels, who was twenty-seven. What were we doing when we were in our late twenties, Matt?'

'Better not to go there.' Matt slipped his pen back into his pocket.

And then he was gone. I called out for my brother. Someone was crying in the next ward.

The Irish nurse was running towards the place where the crying was coming from.

20

The crying was coming from inside me. I was sitting on a chair outside
the physiotherapy room, getting my breath back. I had just finished
my session and discovered I could now walk in a straight line and in
zigzags and backwards and in circles and forwards. I had lost my job.
I was no longer officially a minor historian. Perhaps I was history itself,
flailing around in a number of directions, sometimes all of them at the
same time. While I stared at my feet and rested and wept on the chair,
I became aware there was another pair of feet nearby. These feet were
wearing black sneakers, the laces undone on the right foot. When I
looked up I saw my friend Jack standing over me. His hair was silver
and he wore it in a bun on top of his head. He was wearing the usual
linen jacket over his chinos, his hands in his jacket pockets, a fountain
pen clipped to his top pocket. At the same time the tea lady was wheeling a trolley past the row of chairs outside the physiotherapy room.
She asked if I wanted tea. I shook my head but Jack intervened.

'That will be two cups, thank you.'

He peered at the muffins and scones arranged in a pyramid on the
trolley.

'And two cakes if you'd be so kind.'

He took the cups and scones from her and sat next to me on one
of the plastic chairs.

'Jeeez, Saul!' He bit into the raisin scone and sipped his tea.

We sat in silence while I cried.

The last time I saw Jack was at the French bistro where he had eaten most of my moules and made me pay for the extra bread.

'No,' he said, 'that was not the last time we saw each other.'

After a while he put down his tea and reached for my hand. His was unnaturally warm from holding the plastic cup of tea.

'I am a father now,' I said to him.

'Yes. I know all about that tragedy. It happened a long time ago.'

'Did it?'

'You know it did.'

Jack chewed on his scone and passed me mine.

I did not tell him how Isaac's face came back to me during the long nights in this hospital on the Euston Road. The nights that flowed into post-war East Germany and into twentieth-century Massachusetts and into the house in Bethnal Green and back to West Berlin in 1979 where I bought my father an early edition of *The Communist Manifesto*. I paid for it with all of my student grant. I had no money after that. My brother sent me the train fare to get home from Cambridge when the term ended.

I pushed my scone towards Jack. 'You can have mine as well. I live on morphine.'

'I'm good.' He lifted his left hand and lightly patted his stomach, his right hand still squeezing my hand.

'You know, Saul, I have recently returned from former East Germany. Zwickau, to be precise. It used to be the home of the Trabant factory. I was covering a car fair there for a newspaper. There were quite a few Trabants on display.'

'Yes,' I nodded. 'The Trabant is the East German family car.'

'Well, it used to be,' he said. 'While I was there, I interviewed a young woman who still owned the Trabi that had belonged to her grandfather in the late fifties. It was one of her most treasured possessions.'

'What was her name?'

'I've forgotten. Why do you want to know?'

'Was her name Luna?'

'Oh, I think I would have remembered that name if it was. She was good company.'

Jack started to tell me more about the Trabants on display at the fair.

He made some sort of joke about how the design had never changed.

'You have to understand,' I said, reaching for my tea, which now had a skin of milk settling across the top, 'the West had banned exports of steel to the GDR and it had no reserves of its own. It was an ingenious design. The first vehicle to be made with recycled materials.'

'You are your father's son after all.' Jack squeezed my hand. 'How are you, my friend?'

I wasn't in the mood to talk. The mournful sound of the rubber wheels of the tea trolley squeaking on the lino floor was the right soundtrack for the end of the world. Sometimes the tea lady lost her grip and the trolley hit the corners of the walls and beds. It was the equivalent of waterfalls and parrots in my new terrible world.

'She could deliver the tea in a Trabi,' Jack whispered in my ear. 'At least it had a steering wheel.'

I leaned my head back and rested it on the wall. 'The last time we met, you ate all my lunch and charged me for the extra bread.'

'That wasn't the last time we met. But yes, that day was the start of everything. Do you remember what happened when we got home?'

'No.'

'I threw up because I had eaten the mussels that hadn't opened.'

'You were supposed to be playing tennis.'

'After I'd thrown up I had a shower and went to bed.'

'And I got into bed with you.'

'Yes.'

'I thought you were unloving,' I replied.

'I think I was in those days.'

'Are you with someone now?'

The tea trolley hit the wall again. And again.

'Yes. Very much so. And you, Saul?'

'I have sex all the time but I don't know if it's the sex I had thirty years ago or three months ago. I think I have extended my sexual history across all the time zones, but I did have a lot of sex before the collapse of the Berlin Wall. After that it's a blur but I think I had less sex in social democracies than I did in authoritarian regimes.'

'Hey,' he said, 'get better soon and have more sex.'

After a while he slipped the second scone into his jacket pocket.

'Actually,' he said, 'I meant to say how sorry I am to hear about the death of your father.'

I told him not to be sorry, because my father had died many times. The first time he died was around thirty years ago. I had got used to him dying and coming back to life and then dying again. Jack asked me to explain.

'It's an unconscious thought crime,' I said. 'Stalin knew about those and wanted to assassinate anyone who had them, which is all of us.'

'Yes, well, your father is definitely dead, Saul. And I'm sorry he won't be around to pick apples from our trees.'

I could hear Jennifer talking on the phone in the corridor. She was wearing blue suede sandals and a matching blue trouser suit. She told me she had been in touch with Matt about the funeral arrangements for my father. I told her (again) that my father had died many times before he died. In fact, she had worn that very same blue trouser suit to the funeral the first time he died, around thirty years ago.

'Right.' She didn't look that interested.

'Hello, Jack.'

'Hi, Jennifer.'

They began to whisper to each other as if I weren't there.

Jack was saying odd things that didn't make sense.

'He thinks he is walking.'

Jennifer seemed tearful. I remembered that her own father had died when she was twelve. I meant to say something about that but I didn't know how or where to begin. We had spent a lifetime running away from our love for each other. Instead I asked her about her art.

'Tell me [again] what you did after your graduation show.'

'That was such a long time ago.'

'Was it?'

'Yes,' Jack interrupted. 'Nearly thirty years ago.'

'I was thinking about male beauty when I graduated,' Jennifer said. 'That's because of you. I can't remember that much about it. I was looking at athletes and gods and warriors and hermaphrodites. The boys and men with full pouting lips, thin waists, small penises, oiled hair, delicate toes. And I was looking at Donatello's *David* and I was trying to figure out if the penis is what makes a man a man.'

'I know you liked my penis.'

She laughed. 'I did.'

Rainer was standing next to us.

'I'm sorry to hear about your father,' he said.

'We were just talking about my penis, Rainer.' The sun blasted through the grimy hospital windows. Rainer started to laugh. Jennifer laughed. Jack laughed. Obviously, they were much happier than I was.

Jennifer looked down at my bare feet. Did she want to study the length of my toes and check if they were harmoniously and evenly spaced?

'What I meant to tell you,' she said, 'is that your nephews are here.'

There were two teenage boys in uniform sitting a few chairs along from us. They were playing cards. Jennifer and Rainer disappeared into the wall.

I closed my eyes and searched for my hair so I could touch it. It was a useless search so I touched my knees instead and opened my eyes. Jack's lips were somewhere near my ear, giving me information.

'Their names are David and Elijah.'

'Hallo, Karl Thomas,' I said to the younger boy in German.

'I'm not Karl Thomas. I'm Elijah. Matt's son.'

I switched back to English but I was not in England.

'Shouldn't you be at school?'

'Yes.' The older boy nodded. He was about seventeen.

'Dad made us come to see you.'

'So, Karl Thomas,' I leaned over the chair and saw he had an ace in his hand, 'have you learned your ten commandments for the new socialist human?'

'What's that?'

'Don't you belong to a youth group? The Young Pioneers or the Free German Youth?'

'I'm English,' he said. 'And my name is Elijah.'

'Does your youth brigade help clean up the grounds in run-down blocks of flats? I expect you've been up on the roof doing small repairs.'

'My father does roof repairs.'

The older boy in uniform nodded. His hair was dyed green and his fingernails painted various shades of blue and purple.

'I'm David. What commandments should we have learned?'

' "You shall help to abolish exploitation of man by man." '

'Sounds all right to me.'

I looked at his brother, who was trying to figure out when to strike with his ace.

'Elijah, don't you enjoy the sense of belonging to something bigger than yourself?'

'I'm in a play at school.' My nephew laid down his ace on the seat of the chair and the game was over.

David with the green hair told me they were going to spend the afternoon with their father talking to a man about doves.

'What about doves?'

'For Grandad's funeral.'

'I had a son too. His name was Isaac.'

'We know.'

The boys were trying to be polite. They gathered up the cards and dutifully endured a few more minutes on their chairs. The older one had a tattoo of stars and feathers on his left wrist.

'Do you have any good ideas for a better society, David?'

'We can't find the exit,' Elijah replied.

'What do you think about Britain leaving Europe in the most promising years of your lives?'

Jack pointed to the lift behind the chairs. 'The lift will take you to the exit.'

'That's my friend Jack, by the way.'

They nodded at him. He waved back as if he had known them for years.

I walked my nephews to the lift.

'Doesn't your father mind your green hair and nail varnish?'

'Nope.' David shook his green curls. 'He said he got used to it with you.'

He pressed his painted blue fingernail on the button to call the lift.

I was very pleased to see them. Much more pleased than they were to see me. 'Perhaps we can play cards together one day soon. And give my regards to your mother.'

David with the green hair raised his eyebrow, which he hadn't yet dyed green. 'Okay, we'll see how that goes down.'

'Your lift has arrived,' I said theatrically, as if it were a limousine.

After I said goodbye I walked back to my friend with the silver bun eating my scone.

'Do you have ties, Jack?'

'Do you mean as in a tie and suit?'

'As in family. Are you a brother or uncle or anything like that?'

'Yes.'

'You never talk about your ties.'

'Neither do you.'

'True. I wanted to untie all my ties.'

I rested my head on Jack's shoulder. He stroked my arm and sipped his tea. I felt relaxed in his loving company. He wore an ornate turquoise ring on one of his fingers. Its silver band felt cold and made me shiver as he stroked my arm. His fingernails were bitten down. After a while, he took off the ring and continued to stroke my arm. His hair smelled of woodsmoke. I wanted to sleep on his shoulder, but I feared he might not be there when I woke up.

'When I was twenty-eight I fell in love with a man in the GDR.'

'I know. We often talk about Walter. By the way, I've planted two more apple trees in your Suffolk garden.'

I ignored Jack's attempt to plant himself in my more recent history.

'Walter Müller wore trainers that were not at all trendy. His mousy hair fell to his shoulders. His pale blue eyes were all over me. Surveillance was the air everyone breathed. He watched me all the time for various reasons, but mostly for lust and politics. Jennifer's camera was on me all the time too, even when I slept, especially when I slept, but Walter saw me with his naked eye and he saw everything there was to see in me.'

Jack's new gentle fingers continued stroking my arm. After a while it was he who continued the conversation about Walter, while I listened.

'When he first saw you at the station on Friedrichstraße, he had never seen crazy beauty like yours. He couldn't believe you were real. There you were in front of him, with your *Blade Runner* blue eyes and soft lips. You complained about the trains in Britain.'

'Yes, it was like that.'

'You were pretty much tied up there,' he said.

'I did wear a tie in the GDR,' I recollected. 'I wore a tie when I visited Walter in Berlin last year. Before Britain set about untying its ties with Europe.'

'Yes,' Jack said, 'I drove you to the airport. That was March 2015. I think you were changed by that second meeting with Walter in Alexanderplatz. You were happier when you came home.'

21

I stood by the World Clock in Alexanderplatz at two in the afternoon with Walter.

I was not happy but he was not in the mood to indulge my middle-aged melancholy, though he was not unkind. I explained that I was functioning okay. I could hold a conversation and argue coherently with friends in the pub and walk across town and look respectable. My clothes were clean, no buttons missing on my shirts, no one would know I was indifferent to making it to my sixtieth year. I now lectured on post-communist Eastern Europe. My students could not afford the uncontrolled rising rents in the cities and lived with their ageing parents. Walter had lost some of his hair. It was now cropped close to his head, his face was thinner, he wore spectacles with light aluminium frames.

I looked into his pale blue eyes behind the lenses and glimpsed the spectre of the younger Walter, the man who wore a felt hat when he took me mushrooming near his dacha. He told me how his mother, who was old now, missed her job making fish hooks in the factory. She worked two mornings a week as a receptionist in a nail bar. The two young women from Vietnam who owned the business liked her company. Ursula could give a lecture on Marx and Lenin to every customer waiting for a shellac manicure with acrylic tips and rhinestones, if they had the inclination, and some of them did.

I still desired him. I wanted to touch his stomach and feel him tremble again, but this older Walter was not a man who trembled. That was me.

This time he told me more about what had happened to him when the van stopped by the traffic lights in 1988. Everything I had imagined was true.

If I could have thrown myself under a tram on Alexanderplatz or a car on Abbey Road without being saved from my shame by citizens who thought life should be endured at all cost, I would have done so. The authorities had let him go after two days because they were more interested in Luna. They had put their scant resources into her medical training and did not want her to leave.

When Walter embraced me (I was crying as usual), his arms were not desiring, they were maternal, paternal, perhaps brotherly. It was the embrace of compassion, of pity for my overweight, middle-aged self.

'They would have come for her anyway,' he said sternly. 'They knew she was desperate to leave.'

He wore a heavy coat, the collar trimmed with fur, a smart jacket underneath it. After a while, I reminded him how in the GDR it was hard to get him to put on his clothes.

'You were naked all the time. Swimming in the lake, making coffee, mending the table, frying potatoes.'

'We Germans have never been shy about being naked. But you were shy in this regard.'

'Yes, true.' I touched the top button of his shirt. 'I have always been shy. But now that I have lost my looks I am less shy. It shouldn't work like that, but it does. It is what it is. My body, I mean. Yet, Walter, I think you have become better-looking. You're fit. How come?'

'Healthier food.' When he smiled his teeth were straighter and whiter. 'I've swapped most of the beer for water.'

I asked him if he had a lover.

He glanced at the roll of flesh around my stomach.

'Yes, so does Helga. We are parents to our children. We love each other in that way. And you?'

'On and off.'

'Which of you is more on than off?'

'Jack is on.'

We were silent for a while.

'Is life good for you now, Walter?'

'Yes. Thank you for the question.' He dug into his pocket and took out a miniature plastic replica of one of the GDR watchtowers that were now being sold in the tourist shops.

'I'll give it to Jennifer,' I said. 'She watched me all the time.'

I looked into his eyes and he looked away.

'Yes, I know, Walter. Of course I know. I'm not interested in pointing the finger. It's the better side of my carelessness.'

He shrugged. 'You can go find your file if you want.'

In a way I was interested to know more about it. I asked him what he had written.

'You were more paranoid than the Stasi.' He took off his spectacles and slipped them in his pocket. 'You had a big imagination. You made your hand into a fist and started tapping it against the wall of my mother's apartment. You said you were looking for something but you were not sure what that might be. Was the wall hollow or was it solid? You said this action made you feel important, which made you wonder if you felt unimportant the rest of the time.'

'Yes, I do feel insignificant.'

Walter was laughing like he had in the old Germany when he did not have to work all hours to pay his bills and finding a cauliflower was a good day.

'My English friend,' he said, 'you are only significant if you are significant.'

He looked up at the leaden sky. I followed his gaze. There was nothing to see in the sky. Not even the trail from an aeroplane, or shifting clouds, or birds.

'But I will tell you my conclusion when writing the file. I suggested that although Herr Adler has many psychological problems, he is harmless to other people.'

He was still gazing at the sky.

'The problem with my conclusion,' he said formally, 'is that it was not true.'

'What part of it?'

'That you are harmless to other people.'

He leaned forward and kissed me like a lover under the World Clock as the skateboarders sped past us.

'You still have your lips,' he said, as if he were still taking notes. 'Did you ever write your report on our economic miracle?'

'Yes, I did. I engaged supportively with the realities of life in the GDR.'

He laughed his excellent laugh, head back, new teeth bared; it was very open and sexy.

'You are still crazy.'

'Yes. And uglier.'

'No,' Walter said, 'I can see something of the younger maniac in the older you. You can see something of the maniac wall in the older Berlin.'

Soon I would walk away from the Alexanderplatz of the twenty-first century, past the Currywurst kiosks and fast food shops and drug dealers and buskers. A man was strumming his guitar, which he had plugged into a generator. He was singing about seeing clearly after the rain had fallen. I was not sure I could see anything clearly, never mind feel anything clearly, including the monuments that were supposed to mourn the murdered Jews, the murdered Roma, the murdered homosexuals.

I told Walter I had something for him, too. He watched me dig my hand into the bag that Jack had recently given to me. It was made from jute and other natural fibres. I took out a tin of pineapple and handed it to Walter.

He held it up to the light and read the ingredients.

We both knew he could walk into Aldi or Lidl and buy as many tins of pineapple as he desired.

'You know, I don't eat so much sugar these days.'

I gazed at the World Clock and counted the countries that had been added to it since reunification.

'Walter, did you ever hear from Luna?'

He shook his head.

'Why didn't she take her son with her?'

'It would have been foolish to risk his life. She knew we would give Karl Thomas a home.'

'Is he my son?'

Walter laughed again, as if this were not a question that had any significance. His mood had lifted in the last ten minutes.

'Luna was close to Herman, a radiologist at the hospital where she worked. Sometimes I think she might have been pregnant before you arrived. She was always craving tinned pineapple.'

We stood under the big Berlin sky, looking out at the Japanese noodle bars and trams and at two young girls, perhaps seven and nine, riding their bicycles. One of them wore trainers two sizes too big for her feet. She kept losing her grip on the pedals. Her sister was struggling in a coat that was clearly meant for someone younger. The sleeves came up to her elbows. Three of the buttons were missing. I thought they were refugees because their clothes were not their own clothes. 'Yes,' Walter said, 'we know they would prefer to wear their own clothes and ride their own bicycles and have their mother and father nearby, but war is war.' He tapped my arm and pointed to someone walking towards us in the distance.

A young man in jeans and a T-shirt, perhaps in his mid twenties, carrying a small black dog in his arms, was making his way through the crowds. He wore sunglasses in the rain. We both watched him stroll serenely towards us. His headphones were clipped over his ears as he waved to his uncle, who had been a father to him.

I wondered what I could say that would be worth lifting the headphones off his ears to hear? Attention, Karl Thomas. There will be no wars that will destroy your life as you know it. You will always wear your own clothes, your shoes will always fit your feet and you will never have to sleep in an asylum shelter in a foreign country. A new Europe has been forged. The corpses scattered in the ruins of 1945, the rubble of the smashed buildings, the blown-out windows, everyone on the move in search of home and food and missing people and no one owning up to being the sort of person who would have anything to do with genocide, none of this will ever happen again. Would that be a lie or would it be the truth? Or would it be truth and lie knotted together? What if it was more of a lie than truth? And what if it was absolutely the truth?

I felt that I deserved everything that was coming to me from Karl Thomas, who might or might not be my son.

I heard my own plea in my head. Please, Karl Thomas, do not say, 'I believe you knew my mother.'

He was more or less the age I had been when I first visited the German Democratic Republic, which was living on borrowed time and had dissolved a few months after he was born. If Luna had waited a few more weeks, she might have danced on the Wall in the glare of floodlights from the media crews who were filming that night of 9 November 1989. Perhaps she believed she would be reunited with her son, but that did not happen. Instead, Karl Thomas grew up in a united Germany, separated from his mother. I wanted to tell him how Luna had sung and danced for her freedom that night in the dacha, but I felt unqualified to give him this information, as if I were linking myself to his history when I had not played a part in his life. What was the point in giving him stained, old memories? Would they be a gift or a torment? He was the age that Isaac would have been, had he lived to argue with his parents and wound our pride and make culprits of us both. How could I tell this young stranger that in the month of September 1988 I impregnated one and possibly two women who did not want me in their lives at all. What kind of man would he think I was, and indeed, what kind of man did I think I was?

Karl Thomas lifted his headphones, his left hand resting in the fur of the black dog. He said hello.

I reached out my hand and stroked the black dog in his arms. We stayed like that, all three of us stroking the dog while the rain fell on the solar system floating above the World Clock in Alexanderplatz.

Isaac. Karl Thomas. His hair was as black as mine had once been. It fell in curls to his shoulders. My father also had sooty-black hair in his youth, but he never wore it long to his shoulders, it was a short back and sides all the way to his grave.

When Karl Thomas finally removed his sunglasses, his eyes were bright, clear blue, shocking as a snake bite. I wondered how he would use his extreme beauty, which is always useful and always a burden, sometimes even freakish.

I was just about ready to speak to him, to ask him questions about his life, his friends and where he lived, when I felt a hand on my shoulder.

'We are late for our film,' Walter said. 'We must move swiftly if we don't want to miss the beginning.'

'Don't leave just yet,' I pleaded. 'Life is big and new with you both in it.' But they had made plans and Karl Thomas had to get his dog home first. Walter thought they'd make it if they left right away. They walked off together, the dog more or less in step as they dodged the crowds and traffic.

22

'Yes,' Jack said, 'you and I are free.'

My head was still resting on his shoulder.

'Yes,' I replied, 'we are free of ties.'

He took a small sip of tea. My cheek pressed against his throat.

I wanted him to stay and I wanted him to go.

'Don't historians use contraceptives?'

I had no idea how to endure being free. And everything that comes with it.

'In the early days when we were together, Jennifer used to say I looked more like a rock star than a historian.'

'Yes,' he said, smiling, 'but you were not a rock star. You merely resembled one. I suspect it is hard work being a rock star.'

'Even rock stars have ties.'

I lifted my head and opened my mouth while the nurse fed me cool drops of morphine. Jack chewed on his second scone. After a while I reminded him how I had begged Walter on the steps outside Café Einstein to live with me in Suffolk. And how he'd laughed when I outlined for him the sort of life we could aim for together.

Jack scooped up a strand of his hair and tucked it into his bun.

'You have told me all this.'

'Have I?'

'Yes.' He was still stroking my arm with his new gentle fingers. 'You and I read the *New Yorker* in our armchairs. We wake up together and take it in turns to make toast. Our garden is blooming. The black-berries are ripening.'

Morphine silvered my tongue, lifted it this way and that way. I chased it, trying to bite its ripening into truth, but it was too late.

'Everyone is replaceable,' I said, 'but your love is not the love I want.'

Jack was looking in the direction of the stainless-steel lift. After a while he stood up and I walked him over to it.

'I suppose,' he said, 'it offers me an exit from your cruelty.'

As Jack stepped inside, I noticed the floor was covered with autumn leaves. They crunched under the soles of his black plimsolls and he kicked them away. They reminded me of the leaves that had been swept into two small piles under the trees that lined Abbey Road and how some of them were blowing across the zebra crossing. There was something wrong with the doors of the lift. They closed and then opened again, closed and opened. He glanced at the watch on his wrist. I thought that he was lonely in every time, and so was I.

A plane was looping the loop in morphine's numbing rain.
  Looping in the sky above Britain's food banks and rough sleepers.
  My father was the pilot showing me the view.

Jennifer had not moved from my side. She was searching her bag for a small hairbrush which she said was called a Tangle Teezer. I took it from her and began to brush her hair. It was very calming. She had her back to me as she perched on my bed. Her silver hair came down to her waist. Every brush stroke took a long time. The shadow of my hands in her hair danced across the wall. It was livelier than my feeble fingers, but somehow it gave me courage.

I told Jennifer how her beauty came from all of her and how her talent was bigger than my envy.

She was wearing a green raincoat.

Although she did not reply, I knew she was listening. After a while, I suggested she take another photo of myself crossing the Abbey Road. We would then have two copies, one from 1988 and one from 2016. It would be a stretch of history.

'If it's your last wish, I will take that photograph.'

'It is my first wish,' I replied.

'It's like this, Saul Adler: I've been talking to Jack. He's decided not to take the train back to Ipswich. He's staying in a hotel near the Euston Road so he can be near you.'

'Tell him I'll be home in a week.'

I continued to drag the brush through her hair, but the steady rhythm no longer made me feel calm.

'It's like this, Jennifer Moreau: we were young and clueless and reckless, but I never stopped loving you.'

'It's like this, Saul Adler' – she still had her back to me – 'you were so detached and absent, the only way I could reach you was with my camera.'

The brush fell from my hand. I was very frightened. Of everything. Of everything I felt. Of how my son lifted his hands as he lay in my arms while I sang 'Penny Lane' to him under the blue Suffolk skies. Yes, there is a nurse in the song, Isaac, and a banker and a barber and a fireman. And people are looking at photographs in 'Penny Lane'. Like your mother, your young mother, let her sleep while I hold you, she won't walk away, like I will. I was frightened of the way his fingers pulled at my lips as I sang. I was frightened of everything in the past and whatever was going to happen next. I heard Jack's voice, nearby. His silver hair hung down to his shoulders. He had grown a beard. 'I forgive you for everything and I love you, Saul.'

He told me with his eyes that I would never see the apple trees he had planted in our garden. The fruit would fall in autumn and I would not be there to gather it up. I was deeply grateful for Jack's honest love. It lifted me from the Euston Road to Abbey Road, but I think I was still in my bed when I got there.

25

Jennifer and Rainer were waiting for me at the zebra crossing on Abbey Road outside the EMI studios, the zebra stripes, black and white, at which all vehicles must stop to allow pedestrians to cross the road. I was wearing a white suit and white shoes. It was not lost on me that John Lennon, my childhood hero, was no longer with us. This upset me enough to want to call the whole thing off, but Jennifer insisted we pay attention to the detail of the original photograph. I asked her why she was carrying a stepladder.

'You know why.'

She told me again that was how the original photo was taken in August 1969. The photographer placed the ladder at the side of the crossing while a policeman was paid to direct the traffic. As I was not famous we couldn't ask the police to do that, so we had to work quickly. The original photographer only had ten minutes anyway. She set up the ladder as she had done when I was twenty-eight and she was twenty-three, climbed up it and sorted out her camera.

This time she did not have to keep changing the film.

'Okay,' she shouted, 'put your hands in your jacket pockets, look straight ahead, walk now.'

There were two cars waiting. Rainer held up his hand to keep them there.

I stepped forward on to the zebra and then back again. Rainer and Jennifer yelled at me to get a move on. I was wounded like a soldier, but I had been fortunate never to have to fight in a war. I knew as I took a step across the black-and-white stripes that I was walking across deep time, trying to put myself together again. Jennifer stood on the ladder in her jeans and black silk shirt, a pencil poking out of its pocket, poised and steady in her leather boots, looking through the lens of her digital camera. She shouted at me to focus on crossing the road, but there was so much else going on.

I heard the exuberant sound of the cello in Cape Cod, humming with life, more life, and the hammering of the typewriter in the GDR, which was knowledge expressed in sound telling me that Walter had to save himself by filing reports on someone he found beautiful and desirable.

'Cross the road, Saul.'

I could feel my mother's love nearby and, though I felt betrayed by her death, it moved me forward. I took another step. I could hear the bells of trams in East Berlin and the hooting traffic in West London and the low growling of dogs on the boulevards of Europe, on the porches of America, on the sofas of Britain.

'Cross the road.' Jennifer's lips were close to my ear.

I took another step and kept on walking because there was Luna waiting on the pavement outside the EMI studios.

She was smiling and waving. Luna was carrying a canvas bag and she looked just like she had in 1988.

'Hello, Saul. How's it going?'

'I'm trying to cross the road,' I replied.

'Yes,' she said, 'you've been trying to cross the road for thirty years but stuff happened on the way.'

Jennifer and Rainer were breathing near me. Matthew was there too, and my nephews and Jack and Walter and Karl Thomas.

'East and West are together now,' I whispered to Luna.

'Ah yes,' she said, smiling, 'I have heard about that. The German Democratic Republic is kaput.'

'That was a long time ago.'

'It's true,' Luna said, 'I was not in time with history but blood dries faster than memory. I never made it to Liverpool but you smashed up my *Abbey Road* so I have come to see it for myself.'

I continued walking and when I got very close to the other side I reached out to touch her hand.